FOREVER CURVES
A SINGLE DAD ROMANCE

PIPER SULLIVAN

Copyright © 2021 by Piper Sullivan

All rights reserved.

No part of this book may be reproduced in any form or by any electronic or mechanical means, including information storage and retrieval systems, without written permission from the author, except for the use of brief quotations in a book review.

ENJOY SPICY ROMANCES?

Scan the QR code below to read Safeguarded for FREE Now!

CHAPTER 1
BRENNA

"I'm finally doing it, Jessie May, I'm going on a date." Talking to my younger sister before a big date was kind of a ritual for me, especially when it became clear that I had awful taste in men.

"A date? Seriously? That's great, tell me about this guy."

I sighed and gave myself one final look in the mirror. "That's the thing, I don't know. Not really."

"Come on, Bren. Not another blind date?" Her groan of frustration matched my own when Eva had insisted on keeping the man's identity a secret. "I thought we talked about this."

"We did, but this is different, I swear. Remember how I told you some of the girls here have a matchmaking business? Well I finally broke down and decided to let the professionals handle my love life for a change." Honestly, they couldn't do worse than I did on my own.

"And these professionals decided that hiding the man's identity was prudent? And safe?" Jessie May let out a loud bark of laughter and in my mind's eye I could see her shaking her golden blond curls in disbelief.

"Yeah," I sighed. "I've been mighty picky about their choices so Eva figured I couldn't pre-sabotage if I didn't know much about the guy."

"So you don't know anything about him?"

"Plenty, actually. He fits all my criteria. Tall with broad shoulders, good looking and owns his own business. Not married or divorced. I just haven't spoken to him on the phone."

"Please tell me he's not picking you up!" Though Jessie May was the younger sister, she thought being married with kids made her wise.

"Of course not. I'm meeting him. He'll be wearing a green shirt and holding a purple tulip. How romantic, right? I didn't even tell the girls that was my favorite flower." It was one of the reasons I was so excited to meet this man.

The sound of crying interrupted our conversation and I applied another coating of lipstick, preparing for my sister's next words. "Momma duty calls, sis. Have a good date and call me when you get home."

"I promise. Unless the date goes *really* well." I couldn't help but laugh at her groan of disapproval just before the call ended.

The truth was I had no plans to sleep with this man on the first ate. Now, I was just as liberated as the next modern woman, but in the spirit of getting different results, I wanted to try not jumpin' into the sack with a man just because he had a pretty smile, long muscular legs and broad shoulders.

Call it an experiment if you will, because that's what I

was calling tonight even though Olive and Sophie from Time for Love had called it a new beginning. I had bad luck with relationships, and this guy might be better than my own choices, but chances were slim he was my forever after.

But that didn't stop my heart from fluttering in my chest when I stepped inside the restaurant, a feeling of excitement that had nothing at all to do with the scent of grilled meat and tangy barbecue sauce. It was anticipation. I was actually excited about this date, which increased my nervousness.

I gave my eyes a moment to adjust to the dim lights of the restaurant and slowly scanned all the tables and booths where a single guy sat, my gaze sharpened for all shades of green. "Kelly green. Bold choice." The man had his back to the door, and I wondered if that was an oversight on his part or if he wanted his appearance to be a surprise. Either way, I smoothed my hands down the sides of my black ruffled top and black denim skirt, took a deep breath and made my way to the table. "Purple tulips are my favorite."

The man froze and turned slowly, a wide and all too familiar smile on his face. "So I've heard through the grapevine." Grant Lopez, the hottest single man in all of Pilgrim, turned and nearly leveled me with his dimpled grin. "Brenna, you look gorgeous." He stood and kissed my cheek before helping me into my seat.

I gave him a skeptical look as I sat, enjoying the handsome picture he made in a vibrant green shirt that gave his eyes an emerald green appearance instead of their usual mossy green. "Grant. Why do I feel like this is some kind of set up?"

He shrugged and sat back. "In a way, it is. I knew if you

found out we'd been matched, you'd reject me off the bat. Turns out, Eva thought so too, so it wasn't hard to get her to do things this way."

"Your way you mean," I shot back.

"Same thing," he said in a dismissive tone that was lightened by his playful grin.

"I don't like feeling lied to, Grant." I had a long dating history that was littered with liars, cheaters and thieves and I was trying to break that habit. "But I do love a good barbecue, and that's why I'm staying." That, and no matter how hard I fought it, the chemistry between us was undeniable.

"Whatever the reason you decided to stay, I'm happy to have the prettiest dinner date in the restaurant."

I rolled my eyes. "I already said I was staying, no need to lay it on so thick." I looked good and I knew that, but there were at least four more beautiful women enjoying the barbecue.

Grant's deep laugh sounded, rich and well-used, like he was a man who loved to laugh and did it a lot. "Don't have to lay it on thick when it's the truth. So Brenna, what are we drinking?"

I stared at his handsome face for a long moment, taking in the honey colored skin that made his light brown hair darker and his green eyes brighter. The dimple in his left cheek, was unfortunately, the deciding factor. I was a sucker for dimples, and with Grant sitting right across from me, I couldn't remember why I'd been fighting dating him for so dang long. "Let's start with a shot of whiskey and see what happens."

"A woman after my own heart."

I smiled politely at his words, but I let them roll off my

bare shoulders because it was just a saying, something people said when they had something in common with another person. This was just about a good time.

"Good to know."

We drank whiskey and ate too much barbecue while we both flirted outrageously. So far, it was the perfect date. "You know Brenna, if you really wanted to lose my interest, you should've ordered a salad."

"Ha! All men say that, but they don't mean it. Not usually." I'd heard this line on more than one occasion only to find out six months later that *it wouldn't kill me to order a salad once in a while.*

"Well I mean it, so you can take me at my word."

"Does that mean we have time for dessert?" There was a sundae brownie that was calling my name, and since I didn't eat out at fancy restaurants like this often, I wanted to take full advantage.

"Actually, we don't." Grant sighed, realizing he'd walked himself right into a trap of his own making. "We do, but the second part of the date might not be as fun if you're full of fudge."

He laughed again at my shocked expression. "I've seen you order the fudge croissants at Bread Box at least a dozen times, Brenna."

"Oh. Well, maybe stop being such a stalker?"

Another rich, textured laugh that sent a shiver straight through my body. "I prefer to think of it as observant."

And dammit, I liked the thought of being observed by

him. "I'll go freshen up, then, but this next stop better be worth skipping fudge for."

"It will be. I promise."

I took promises from men with a grain of salt but my heart pitter-pattered with excitement as I slicked on more Red Red Wine lipstick and gave my blond hair a much needed fluff. So far I had no complaints about the date or my companion. Grant was intense with his interest but otherwise easygoing, which was pretty damn irresistible in my book.

This is just a date. Only a date. I needed the reminder, especially when I found him waiting for me with a dark, sultry stare as I sauntered back to the table. "Ready?"

"I was born ready, sweetheart. The question is, are you?" He stepped in real close and I could smell the masculine scent of his cologne mixed with the hint of something I just knew was pure Grant aroma.

I swallowed the lump that had formed in my throat and took a step back. "Only one way to find out."

He smiled as if my answer pleased him and put one scorching hand to the small of my back to guide me from the restaurant. "Follow me."

With that deep voice of his, I would probably follow him anywhere. But where he took me next, my absolute favorite thing in the world to do other than hair, sent my desire for him soaring to new heights. "Line dancing. How'd you know?"

"You really want to know?" His lips trembled with amusement. "Every time I pass by your salon, you're dancing. Cutting hair? Dancing. Shampooing or curling hair? Still dancing. Must be why you have such great legs."

Oh damn, I am in serious trouble. Grant wasn't just gorgeous and charming, he was a man who paid attention. I stuck one leg out and twisted my foot left and then right. "These old things? I've had them for years."

"Good," he purred in my ear as he reached for my hand on the edge of the dance floor and tugged me to the middle of the room. "That means you've had plenty of years to practice. Show me what you've got, beautiful."

I tossed my head back and laughed. "Me? Show me what you've got, Yankee."

"Who said I was a Yankee?" Grant wasn't offended which was just another point in his favor as he twirled me around the floor with ease, his steps graceful and confident.

The first song ended with us chest-to-chest and I gasped at just how close we were and how hard his body was, everywhere. "Mostly your accent, but I'm sure I could think of a few more things after a few more dances."

His smile brightened at that and I pressed against him. "Guess I better not disappoint."

"Guess so," I told him as another song started. Grant's hands never left mine and I had a feeling I was going to do something really stupid, like sleep with him, which was exactly what Eva had warned me not to do. But dang, he made it hard to be a good girl the way he kept that heated green glare on me, smiling at me like I really was the prettiest girl in the whole place.

Four, maybe five songs later and we were both damp with sweat, breathing hard and smiling like fools. I could see us this same way only in a whole other setting and I had to look away as I sipped my ice cold lemonade. "Another dance?"

I didn't answer, just put my hand in his and let him guide me to the dark end of the dance floor as a slow country ballad started up and Grant pulled me close. So close that I could feel his heart beating against my chest.

"You're a good dance, Brenna."

"So are you," I whispered in his ear, enjoying the way his breath hitched at that one little move. "You impressed me."

"Yeah?" I nodded and he leaned in closer. "Then I already consider tonight a win."

I knew the kiss was coming, I could just feel it based on the heat in his eyes and the way he licked his full lips a moment before they pressed against mine. His lips were soft and pillowy, but they were also firm and insistent, almost commanding as his tongue slid back and forth across the seam of my lips until I opened up. Grant moaned and his grip tightened on my hips, letting me feel just how much he was impacted by the kiss.

The kiss was soft and gentle, but it was hot enough to singe the material right off the lacy black panties I'd worn to boost my confidence. "Wanna get out of here?"

This was it, the moment of truth. Was I gonna to be a good girl? A grown woman who made good decisions, or was I going to live in the moment and satisfy my desire for this man who had intrigued me for weeks? "I think I do." I still hadn't made up my mind and Grant didn't push.

"You think?" Like the gentleman he was, Grant wasn't halfway to the door to force the issue, he kept swaying to the music and he still held me close.

Ah, hell. Who am I kidding? I nodded, my decision firm in my mind now. "I want to get out of here."

His shoulders sagged in relief and I grinned. "Your place or mine?"

My grin broadened at his question. "Depends on who makes it to the street first. Race ya!" I took off at a run, thankful I'd worn my favorite pair of boots tonight instead of the sexy stilettos Jessie May had insisted I wear.

CHAPTER 2
GRANT

Damn, was there anything hotter than a woman who wasn't afraid to laugh out loud? Yeah, a woman who did what it took to win without worrying about a man's ego. It was hot as hell watching her race to her car, long shapely legs pumping hard until I lost sight of her.

Yeah, Brenna McKenna had my blood all fired up with her thick country twang, quirky sayings, and most of all, that tiny denim skirt she wore that had me thinking dirty thoughts about her from the moment she arrived at the restaurant. I never thought I had a thing for cowgirls until I met this brash blond, but dammit, I liked her a lot. She was all legs and tits and hair, and those were three of my favorite things in the world. She also possessed another trait that was at the top of my list, she was a woman who was up for a good time.

Only a good time.

The gift certificate for Time for Love was meant to be a

joke from Miles and Liam, but I wasn't a man to be outdone, so I'd gone in and taken the classes and got matched. With Brenna. Did I also mention that my middle name was Lucky?

I slammed on my brakes in behind Brenna's salon and killed the engine as she stood at a heavy steel door, keys poised to unlock. "Damn woman, do you moonlight as a street racer?" Not that it wasn't hot as hell to see her drive fast and handle the car with ease, but a man could only be so turned on before things got tricky.

"Not these days," she said vaguely and unlocked the door.

"That sounds like a story I have to hear."

My gaze focused on her heart-shaped ass as we climbed the long staircase that led to the apartment above the salon. Her legs were long and shapely, proving she was a woman who worked as hard as she played and my fingers itched to reach out and touch her.

All too soon we reached the top of the stairs and Brenna gripped the doorknob before she turned to me, a smile on her face, blond brows arched in question. "Story time or sexy time?"

That was an easy answer, but I didn't do most things easily, so I leaned in and tucked a strand of blond hair behind her ear. "All of your time with me is sexy time." Before she could tell me how cheesy the line was—which I already knew—my lips were on hers but this wasn't like the hot but publicly appropriate kiss that I'd given her at the dance club. No, this was a closed door kiss that started of slow and sweet, because I knew how to be short and sweet, especially when it fired a woman up to long and hot and lasting all night.

Brenna wrapped her arms around my neck and pushed her curves against my body, moaning as I deepened the kiss, squirming as my hands slid from her waist to her round ass and squeezing tight. *Holy shit*, she had curves for days, which I already knew because she favored figure-hugging clothes most of the time, but I had no idea how soft and luscious they were until this very moment.

"Grant," she whispered against my lips as one leg hitched up over my hip, bringing her hot center up close and personal with the erection trying hard to break through the zipper of my pants.

"Tell me what you want, Brenna."

She smiled at my words and jumped in my arms, wrapping her legs around my waist before her lips crashed to mine. On the second go round, the kiss was hotter and hungrier, a hell of a lot more intense, I reached blindly for the door knob and pushed into her apartment. She pushed the door closed and I pressed her back against the door, eager to get another taste of her lush mouth while I had her in my arms, squirming against my cock.

Her lips tasted like cherries and whiskey, and her ass was a perfect fit for my hands. So was her narrow waist and those plump tits. In fact, everywhere my hands roamed, her body fit perfectly, a thought that sent more fire raging through my veins.

"Holy hell!" Brenna let out a nervous laugh as she pulled back and smacked her head against the door. "You are six feet of trouble Grant Lopez."

I smiled and nipped her bottom lip. "Wrong, sweetheart.

I'm six feet two inches of pleasure." My thumbs grazed over her nipples, hard through her shirt and her bra.

"Oh!" Her head fell back again, exposing her throat to me and I licked the long column of her neck until she moaned and her eyes fluttered closed. The scent of her perfume was stronger from the exertion of dancing all night and it only made me want to taste more of her. "Grant," she moaned my name and gripped my shoulders as she unwrapped her legs and let her feet fall to the floor.

I stayed close, pressing my hips against her, but fully prepared to take a step back and head home to a cold shower, Brenna was a good country girl after all. Her blue gaze was so dark it was damn near black as she stared at me, her lips shiny as they stretched into a sultry grin. "I love to hear you moan my name."

"You do have a knack for making me moan," she said and then reached for the hem of the sexy off-the-shoulder shirt that had been driving me crazy all night, and pulled it over her head, leaving her in nothing but a lacy black bra that did nothing to conceal her pretty pink nipples. "I like that about you."

"Yeah? That makes us a pretty good team, I'd say." My tongue traced the edge of her bra, drawing a breathless moan from Brenna's plump lips. Her bra was in the way and I made quick work of it, too hungry for that dusty pink nipple to wait.

"Yeah," she said on a strangled groan as her fingers tangled in my hair. "Hell yeah."

I smiled around her nipple, sucking a little harder just to see what sound she would make next. I was rewarded with a low growl as I moved to the other breast, pinching the already damp one which drew another low moan from her. I kissed my way from her tits down to her slim waist where she was all soft, curvy woman. My fingers worked quickly to get the tiny skirt off and I tossed it behind me. "Good?"

Brenna nodded and smiled down at me. "Good and hot."

I stared at the lace panties she wore. When I turned her around, I saw that the sexy little shorts cut through her plump ass cheeks, and the sight made my mouth water. I gave her cheek a smack and she gasped with pleasure. My tongue found her hot and damp through the panties, and she let out a shuddery sigh. For long minutes I kept her like that, facing the door while I gripped her ass cheeks and licked from behind over her panties.

Brenna shook and trembled. "Grant," she panted and I turned her back to face me, tugging the lacy panties over her hips and down her legs with my teeth. "Mmm, dirty."

"You impressed yet, Brenna?" I was close enough to see the glisten on her swollen clit and I knew she could feel my hot breath between her warm thighs.

She laughed and threw one leg over my shoulder. "I'm fixin' to be real impressed, as soon as you get down to business."

My cock twitched at her command, and I leaned in until the tip of my tongue slid between her thick bare lips and her hips bucked forward. On and on I licked and sucked, teasing Brenna with my mouth until she fell apart and her sweet honey coated my tongue.

Her legs shook and I picked her up, held her mostly naked body in my arms. "Bed? Sofa? Shower?"

Brenna laughed and wrapped her arms around my neck.

"I'm so impressed that I'm just gonna say yes, Grant. Hell yes."

We started on the sofa before making our way to the bedroom and sometime, just before the sun came up, we said a long hot goodbye in the shower. Twice.

CHAPTER 3
BRENNA

"Remember, The Big Tease is always here for your hairstylin' needs!" I waved off a couple of new customers who'd driven all the way from Tulip just to get their hair done by yours truly. They both wore satisfied smiles as they talked about wowing their friends with their new looks.

When the women were gone, I dropped down into one of my chairs to catch my breath. One of the stylists had decided to skip town to visit her boyfriend in Louisiana, which left me handling double the customers, and it seemed like every woman in Texas wanted her hair done today. Business was good and I would never complain about that, but I was exhausted in the best way possible.

And that thought took me back a few days to the last time I was pleasantly exhausted and aching all over. *Grant*. That was, hands down, the hottest one night stand of my entire life. The man knew how to please a woman and he was eager to please, something I've always appreciated in a guy. My legs were shaky for a day or two afterwards, and even now, just the memory of the way he'd taken me with his mouth up against the door, was enough to get me all hot and bothered.

Luckily my afternoon appointments started to arrive, sixty year old best friends who came every other week for the full salon gossip experience. "Barbara and Duffy, how are you ladies doing?"

Barbara waved off the question. "We're fine. What we want to know is who put that big grin on your face? Spill, honey."

Oh there was no way in hell I was spilling the details of my date with Grant. It was too fun and too special to ruin by sharing. I wanted to think of that night untainted by expectation or gossip.

"I'll give you an extra three minutes of scalp massage if you change the subject."

Barbara smiled and shook her head. "I have a massage in two days so get to talkin' honey." She took a seat in an empty chair and I grabbed two smocks to drape across the women. "We're waiting. Let a couple of old ladies live vicariously through you."

"I'm just happy that business is going so well," I told her. "New business don't often do well, but thanks to customers like you ladies, my business is boomin'."

"Bull hockey," Duffy said, disappointment heavy in her voice.

The bell over the door sounded and I sighed, hoping I wouldn't have to turn away a walk-in. "Be with you in a moment," I called out as the sound of high heels sounded on my hard floors. Something told me not to turn around, but I was never good at listening to my instincts, no matter how hard I tried. "Sophie. Olive. Hey."

"Don't you hey us," Olive said, hands resting on top of her pregnant belly. "We came to see how your date went."

"Oh, a date," Duffy said in a sing-song voice.

"I knew there was a reason," Barbara added with a smile.

I sighed, ignoring the old women in favor of the younger women with the expectant looks aimed in my direction. "I haven't even had time to process how it went yet."

"It's been three days, and *I think* we've been patient." Sophie didn't mince her words and her matter-of-fact tone said she wouldn't be deterred easily. "How did it go?"

"It's been six months," Barbara said, her tone letting me know exactly how pathetic she thought that was. "It's about time."

"Good for you, getting back out there," Duffy said, her tone almost not at all condescending.

I sighed and sent a glare towards both older women. Okay, fine, it had been a long damn time since I went out on a date, but in my defense my ex did a good job of souring me on the notion of love and relationships. I still was, despite using a matchmaker. But living in a small town where all of your friends were startin' to couple up, meant I had to at least try to get back out there. Didn't it? "They're all liars, why should I line up for that circus again?" If a man was a liar, a thief or a cheater, chances were good that I would fall for him.

"But that's not Grant," Olive insisted. "You came to us so we could weed out the jerks and the liars and the psychopaths, so trust the process."

"And if you can't trust the process, trust us," Sophie added with a scowl. "The algorithm works. And Grant *is* a good guy."

I wanted to believe that, because everything I knew of him so far said he was a good man. But he was also too pretty and too charming, and guys like that couldn't keep it in their pants. They couldn't resist using their looks and their charms to manipulate, to cheat. Then again, was I searching for fidelity? Maybe, but maybe what I should be searching for is fun.

Grant had that in spades.

"The date went well," I finally relented. "We had barbecue and went line dancing, so it's safe to say that we both had a good time." The fact that they'd found me a man who could dance was a point in their favor and I wasn't afraid to tell them so. "Good job, ladies. It was a good match."

"Was?" Olive leaned forward, staring at my face to see if I was lying or holding back. I hoped she had no idea I was doing a little bit of both. "What's that mean?"

Sophie wore her skepticism like an expensive accessory. "Do you plan on seeing Grant again? Have you set up your second date?"

And that was the other reason I wasn't ready to proclaim Grant Lopez a good guy. After a date that fun and a night that ended so well, what kind of man wouldn't call after that? A player, that's who. "We didn't talk about it." Not between rounds of sex, and not during the long hot make out session at the door before we said goodbye.

Olive sighed, annoyed. "So, it was just one date and you're done?"

"I don't know. We didn't talk about a second date." *Probably because you gave it up on the first night.* At least that's what Jessie May would have said if I'd told her how the night ended, which I hadn't. Yet. Maybe that's why he didn't call, and if that was the case, I decided I was all right with that. I didn't want a guy sticking around just waiting to get laid.

Sophie sighed and stepped in close, staring me right in the eyes. "Would you go out with Grant again, if he asked?"

"I don't know. Maybe." Definitely.

I should have giving my answer more thought, because the shared smile between Olive and Sophie sent a stab of fear through me. They were up to something, I just knew it. "Perfect," Olive said and turned on her heels.

"We'll be in touch," Sophie said, almost as if they were sharing a thought. "Have a good day ladies." She gave a short finger wave to the rapt audience that was Barbara and Duffy, before following Olive out.

"Grant? That hunky new guy who works at the bodyguard school?" Duffy clapped her wrinkled hands excitedly. "Tell us everything. That man flirts so well, I can only imagine the things he can do naked."

"Duffy!"

"What? I'm old, not dead. And I have a very active imagination," she said around a laugh as she wiggled her eyebrows.

"Too active sometimes, if you ask me," Barbara added with a grumble.

"No one asked you, Babs." Duffy laughed again before her gaze, and then Barbara's, zeroed in on me. Expectant.

"He can dance," I offered with a hesitant smile, thankful that the mention of a man who can dance sent the conversation hurtling into another direction.

CHAPTER 4
GRANT

"Good job today, guys. Rest up, because the afternoon course is twice as hard." This week's group was a bunch of new retirees gearing up for their first jobs in personal security, and we were all determined to make sure they were prepared. Over prepared.

"Twice as hard for you, *maybe*. Old man." I didn't see who said it, but I could guess.

"Don't let this handsome mug fool you, Kirkland, I can still kick your ass." The rest of the guys laughed and 'ohhed' as guys tended to do when they got together. "Don't forget to hydrate."

"Yes sir!" Old habits died hard, so I didn't bother telling them to just call me Lopez. Again.

I shook my head and made my way to the small office that had been set aside for me. I didn't need much room for files and papers, and mostly I just used the gymnasium to plot out my obstacle courses. But some parts of the job required a desk and a computer, so that's where I was headed when a pair of heels click-clacking on the hard floors stopped me in my tracks. I turned slowly and saw Eva marching towards me, an angry vision in red. "Eva! To what do I owe the pleasure of this visit?"

"Don't you flash that dimple at me, Grant Lopez." She pointed one long red nail in my direction and I took a step back.

"What are you talking about?"

She sucked in an outraged breath as if I was some kind of mind reader or something, glancing left and then right, like all of sudden she was worried about privacy. "I'm talking about, *Brenna.*" She whispered the name as if I couldn't figure out why she ambushed me at the office.

"I figured that much. What's the problem?" We hadn't talked about it, but there was an unspoken agreement between us to keep our night together between us. Just the two of us. I nodded for Eva to follow me inside.

"The problem is, Grant, that it's been more than a week and you've kept us hanging. More importantly, you've kept Brenna hanging."

What? "Did she say something to you?" Brenna was a straightforward woman, it was one of her top ten qualities, and I was sure, relatively sure, that she would come to me directly if she had a problem with me.

"No, of course not," she said dismissively. "You know that's not Brenna's style. I'm here in a professional capacity." She gave me a haughty look. "How was the date?"

"It was fine. We had a good time, a very good time."

Eva huffed out a laugh and shook her head. "That's exactly what she said." And apparently it wasn't an acceptable answer, because she leaned over my desk, glaring at me until she had my full attention. "So why haven't you or Brenna set up a second date?"

That was a good question, and one I had no answer to. "I don't know. Maybe we've both been busy with work, Eva, I can't really say."

"You can't or you won't?" One black brow arched in question.

I sighed and fell back against the plush desk chair. "I don't know, Eva. I really can't say."

"I don't believe you."

"Well I'm not in the habit of proving myself when I don't have to, so is there anything else?"

"Nothing at the moment," she said and stared at me for a long moment, and I stared back to let the little spitfire know that she couldn't intimidate me. "I'll be talking to you soon, Grant. Real soon." She marched off and I stayed in my seat until the sound of her angry footsteps faded into nothingness.

"Is it safe?" Liam stuck his head in my office, a crooked grin on his face.

"Safer than it was a few minutes ago. Coward."

Liam shrugged. "Not a coward, just a man with a strong sense of survival. What did you do to piss her off, anyway?"

"Apparently Brenna and I aren't moving fast enough for the Time for Love ladies and they're desperate to know why." I did have a good reason for not asking Brenna out again, but it was none of their business.

"Why are you dragging your feet?" Liam held up his hands in a defensive posture when I glared at him. "I'm not asking for Olive, just my own curiosity."

"Don't know. I've been busy, and she runs her own business. Time is limited, I guess."

"Bull. You're lying and I can't figure out why."

"Why what?" Miles appeared in the doorway, a harried smile on his face.

"Why Grant is dragging ass to get a second date with Brenna."

Miles perked right up at that news and strode inside, taking the seat beside Liam. "Why?"

"Says they're both busy," Liam answered for me. "I think that's crap."

"Definitely crap," Miles agreed. "I think he's scared."

"I'm not scared," I growled at them. "And I'm also sitting right here! So stop talking about me like I'm not in the room."

They snickered like little girls, and I rolled my eyes. "If you're not scared, what is it then? Is she a bad kisser?" Liam asked, laughing.

"Oh shit, maybe *you're* a bad kisser, and that's why she isn't itching for a second date."

I thought about those kisses, on her mouth and all over the rest of her, and that definitely wasn't the reason neither of us had pulled the trigger. But what was Brenna's reason?

"Well, it wasn't bad kisses based on that look," Liam said with another laugh.

"Did either of you need something?" If I let them continue to speculate, they would eventually get the truth out of me and I wasn't ready to share.

"Nope, I just came to see what you did to piss off Eva."

"I need something," Miles' smile was wide, but there was suddenly tension in his shoulders. "From both of you."

Liam and I groaned simultaneously. "What is it?"

"Nothing big, just my engagement party. I need some help."

"Help?" Liam and I spoke at the same time. "What kind of help? Because I don't do balloons or streams or whatever."

Miles barked out a laugh. "We're two adults starting a family, there won't be any balloons, Liam. At least, I don't think so." He sighed. "Honestly I have no clue what the hell goes into planning an engagement party, but Shannon wants one, and she's too pregnant to do it all on her own."

"Been there," Liam grumbled. "Still living it every damn day."

"Maybe stop getting your wife pregnant every ten months?" He rewarded me with a middle finger of friendship.

"Maybe stop being afraid to call a pretty woman, and then I'll take relationship advice from you."

Ouch. "So Miles, about this party?"

Liam snickered.

Miles glared at Liam and let out a slow breath. "Planning meeting tonight. I'll provide the food, but bring your own booze. My backyard at eight." With that Miles walked out, probably off to sign up a bazillion more clients to come to Pilgrim and get put through physical hell.

"I guess we have plans tonight. Think he'll bring tacos?"

Liam stood and shrugged. "Maybe someone should see if Shannon is in the mood for tacos tonight?"

I smiled. "Excellent idea."

"And while you're at it, you can pump her for information on Brenna."

"Dick," I growled and tossed my stylus at him, but his quick reflexes meant it sailed right into the hallway. I reached for my phone the moment it pinged with a message. I groaned. It was Eva.

Reservations at Tomahawk Sushi. Tomorrow night. Eight-thirty. Make sure Brenna is available. And interested.

CHAPTER 5
BRENNA

"Sushi? You brought me to a sushi joint?" I didn't mean to sound so horrified, really I didn't, but raw fish? On a date? Or period? It was literally, the worst date I could imagine, which was really a letdown after the first one.

"You don't like sushi? Who doesn't like sushi?"

"Me! I don't even like raw vegetables and you expect me to eat raw fish and other sea creatures?" I sounded shrill, I knew that, but the idea of eating octopus tentacles or some other weird shit was really causing me to panic. I shook my head, hoping the force of the motion would propel the car to any other place where there was food.

Grant laughed beside me and dropped a hand on my leg, but not even the feel of his strong grip on my thigh could get me moving. "Come on, Brenna, just give it a try."

"I have. Once upon a time I dated a guy, one of those cosmopolitan types, you know? Anyway he convinced me to try sushi and against my better judgment, I did. You know what happened, Grant? Do you?"

"What?"

"I tossed my cookies. Right there in the dining room of the restaurant, I let it all go. It was mortifyin'!" I don't know which was worse, the puke or the texture of raw fish.

When he started to laugh, I lifted my head and glared at him. "I'm not laughing at you, I swear. It's just...wow."

"Yeah, I know! Now you see why I can't go in there."

"I don't see that at all. Come on." Before I could repeat my objections, the handsome jerk got out of the car and jogged around the front until he stood outside the passenger door. "I promise you'll like it and if you hate it, there's plenty of cooked dishes. I already checked."

That stopped me in my tracks. "You did?"

"Yep. There's miso soup and tempura veggies, they even have like four types of teriyaki. So, are we going inside?"

How could I say no now, when he went through the effort of making sure the menu was versatile just in case his date was a head case? I nodded. "Yeah, okay. We're going inside." I put my hand in his and smiled. "Lead the way."

The restaurant had a funky vibe to it, very much a sushi joint in the heart of Texas. There were tomahawks and cowboy hats hanging on the wall, and what I suspected was country music in Japanese blasting through the speakers. "First impressions?"

"Colorful. Eclectic."

"Quirky enough for you to give this place a proper chance?"

I nodded. "Yeah."

"Good." He kept his hand on mine as we followed the hostess to a small table near the center of the restaurant. Even with the table between us, Grant's masculine scent left me too distracted to look at the menu because all of my focus was on his rugged features and full lips, and that dimple that made an appearance every time he bit his lip, twisted his mouth left or right, and most of all, when he smiled. "That all right with you?"

"What? Sorry."

He smiled like he knew I found him far more interesting than anything on the menu. "I just asked if you know what you want?"

You. "I'll have some soup and the tempura platter."

"And you'll try some of the sushi, if I ask really nicely?"

My mouth opened to say no, but instead curved into a smile. "How nicely are we talkin'?"

Grant's grin lit up the whole restaurant. "I guess we'll just have to wait and see, won't we?"

I did my absolute best to stop the knife of electricity that zipped through me at his words and the heated look he sent across the table, but that tiny twitch of his lips told me I'd failed. "We have to start with sake, right? When in Rome and all that."

The sake arrived at the table in a decorate carafe with two small matching glasses. Our waitress poured the first two drinks, all fancy like, and I sat back and enjoyed the process, kind of like the first time I watched my instructor give a girl highlights. Grant held the small cup in the air, a panty melting smile on his face. "To new friends and trying new things."

"I'll drink to that." The sake was pretty good, better than I remembered anyway, then again, I tried to block that date out of my memory completely. "So Grant, tell me something about yourself."

"What would you like to know, Brenna?" The way he said my name, like it was the name of some exotic princess from the romance novels I read when I had a chance, never failed to produce a physical reaction.

I wanted to know everything right up front to see if Grant Lopez was as good as he seemed, but that was bad date etiquette, so I started with the easy questions first. "Tell me about your family."

His smile brightened at the mention of his family and dammit, who could find fault with a man who lit up when he thought of his family. "I have two brothers, twins and older than me by about six years. Casper is an ER surgeon and Vance is an environmental lawyer. They both live in Boston, not too far from where we grew up."

"Holy crap, talk about a family of high achievers. Your folks must be pleased as punch with how you all turned out." It was kind of disappointing to learn he was out of my league, but that fact also allowed me to relax a little more.

Grant shrugged it off like it was no big deal. "Being in the military isn't quite the same as emergency surgery, or suing big corporations who pollute local waters, is it?"

It wasn't all that ladylike, but I had to snort at his ridiculous statement. "You're kiddin' me, right? Navy SEALs are like a military Ph.D., aren't they with all that specialized training? You guys are the baddest of the bad asses."

"Wow. Been doing your homework?" Before I could answer, the waitress arrived with enough food, it seemed, for five people. My soup and tempura came along with two long plates filled with sushi. "So, tell me what else you learned to impress me, Brenna."

I laughed and kept my gaze trained on the sushi while he added green gloop to the soy sauce with his chopsticks. "Not to impress you, actually. I love romance novels and romance writers love sexy military guys and apparently none are sexier than SEALs." He laughed again and I glared at him. "That's not me saying you're sexy or anything."

"Of course not." He held up a piece like an expert with those little wooden sticks, about two inches from my mouth. "Open up."

"What is it?" It looked like bacon and smelled like barbecue sauce, but neither of those were likely.

"Unagi roll," he said simply and brought the roll closer. "You know you want to open up."

I debated it for a long moment before I relented. "What the hell. Won't be the first time I embarrassed myself on a date." I closed my mouth around the bit and chewed slowly, hesitantly but deliberately until it was gone. "Not bad. What is unagi?"

"Eel."

I quickly reached for my sake cup and drank the whole thing, inelegantly but it was enough to wipe the image of a slithering black eel from my mind. "It was...good, but eel? Seriously?"

Grant laughed and reached for the second eel roll, dipping it in the soy sauce mixture as if he ate sushi all the time. "What about you, Brenna, tell me about your family?"

I told him all about Jessie May. "She's two years younger than me, but because she married her high school sweetheart and is well on her way to a brood of children, she thinks she's a decade wiser than I am." She might be right, but that was a secret between me and god. "We're close though. She's probably my best friend."

"She doesn't live in Pilgrim?"

I blinked, confused. "I'm not from Pilgrim either. She lives in Louisiana, just outside Baton Rouge."

"So you're from Louisiana. Do they have cowgirls in Louisiana?" Before I could answer, he held up another roll, this one with tiny orange balls in the center.

"What is that?" It was fishy as hell and I needed more sake to fortify myself.

"It's salmon. You'll like it. I promise." He dipped it in soy sauce and brought it back to my lips.

I wasn't sure if I would like it as much as I liked the attention Grant lavished on me, taking care to feed me each piece like it mattered to him that I liked the food. But I accepted the roll and chewed slowly again, but this time it was due to the weird texture of the balls popping in my mouth. "Weird. But not as revoltin' as I thought it would be."

He laughed. "Not exactly the compliment I was hoping for, but it's a start."

"Not like any salmon I ever had."

"Its salmon wrapped around salmon roe. Fish eggs."

"Oh, gross!" I reached for the sake again and stopped myself, reaching for the glass of water instead. "Why in the hell do people eat fish eggs?"

"They don't have fish eggs in Louisiana?"

"I'm from Texas!"

"Ah, good to know. Ready for another one? This one is just tuna, I promise."

Tuna. I could do tuna. I hoped. "Oh fine."

"Where in Texas are you from?"

"A small town near the border. Our parents retired and up and moved to Florida, so I haven't been back in years, but I'm a Texas girl." The tuna roll was my favorite with the creamy avocado mayo that had something spicy in it.

"I knew you were a real-life cowgirl. It's the accent. And the hair. And the tight jeans."

"You have a thing for cowgirls, Grant?"

"Never had before," he said and dipped the second tuna roll before he held it up to my lips. "But I definitely have a thing for one particular cowgirl."

Holy hell. "Are you for real?"

He blinked at the question. "What do you mean?"

"I don't know. You seem too good to be true, so I'm asking, are you for real? Do you mean what you say?"

"Always." He held up another roll and I knew what it was immediately.

"Nope. Those suckers are too smart to eat, he'll probably find a way to wiggle out of my mouth while I sleep." He shrugged and ate the octopus pieces. "You know they can open jars, right? Jars, Grant!"

He shrugged. "I know that now, which kind of makes it hard to enjoy the second one." But he did, popping it in his mouth like candy. "So, what's the verdict on second chance sushi?"

I thought about my answer carefully as he stole a tempura asparagus from my plate, crunching wildly. "Much better the second time around. The company too." I still wasn't sure if Grant was for real, he was too handsome and charming to also be a guy who cared about making sure his date enjoyed herself, both in and out of the sack.

"Cheers, then. To another successful date."

It was a good date, a damn good date. "Cheers."

We drove to the river to walk after dinner, enjoying the stars twinkling in the sky and the slow slog of the water to our left. "There's a place up ahead that has the best fried ice cream I've ever tasted. Want to share some fried ice cream balls with me?"

More food? "Absolutely. As long as you know that there's no way I'm getting naked for anyone after all this food." I could already feel my stomach poking out more than I would like, and I sent up a silent thanks to Eva who'd encouraged me to go with a flowing top.

Grant stopped walking and turned to face me, his moonlit face relaxed into a smile as he leaned forward and pressed a kiss to my cheek. "That's okay, I'll just have to get you naked another night."

Hot damn! I was pretty sure that by the time he dropped me off at home and kissed me senseless, I had a big ol' crush on Grant.

CHAPTER 6
GRANT

"It's about damn time you guys showed up." I was on my third cup of coffee by the time Miles and Liam made it for our meeting at Bread Box.

Liam smiled through his grunt and dropped down into one of the small bistro chairs. "Maybe if you had a woman to warm your bed, you'd understand how difficult it is to leave in the mornings."

"Speaking of, how was your date with Brenna?" Miles took the empty seat that faced the register, so he could flash goofy grins at his woman the whole time.

"It was fine. And why are you late? Shannon's been here since I got here."

"So, the date?"

I glared at Liam. "Are you really interested, or are you doing recon for Olive?"

He shrugged. "A little of both, I guess. Did you bomb again?"

I shook my head. "You two are like the gossiping old

ladies who run this town."

Miles threw his head back and laughed. "This is what passes during the day for small town entertainment so get used to it. And tell us how it went."

How did the date go? "It started out rough when I pulled into the parking lot of Tomahawk Sushi." They laughed until they cried while I recounted our conversation in the car, including Brenna's failed sushi date. "But I got her inside and we had a good time. Really good. She's nice and gorgeous, and she is always a good time. What's not to like?" Best of all, Brenna didn't seem to be hunting for a husband. Or forever. "And that's all I'm saying before you start planning my wedding."

"You're safe with us," Miles assured me. "I'd be more worried about Sophie, Eva and Olive."

"Yeah," Liam agreed. "They've been on a roll lately and won't let anything stop them, so if you're not looking for love, back away slowly."

Shannon stopped at the table, with an affectionate smile as she rubbed her big pregnant belly. "Hey babe," she cooed and leaned in for a kiss that had Miles smiling like a fool in love. "Hey guys."

"Looking good, Shannon." She was one of those women who looked good pregnant, all glowing and happy, which probably had to do with her impressive cleavage.

"Thanks, Grant." Her smile lingered on me, but not in a flirtatious kind of way, more like a knowing way. As if she *knew* something, which made me wonder what Brenna had told her about me. About us. "As handsome as you boys are, you need to buy something or clear out." She sauntered off with a cute little finger wave.

"I know what that look means," Miles said. "Even if Shannon won't admit it or answer any of my questions."

I didn't care what she knew as long as she kept it to herself. "I like your woman more each day," I told him and stood to order our breakfast, which mostly consisted of too much coffee.

"Next!" Mara's familiar bark never failed to bring a smile to my face, and the bored look she sent me as I approached the counter actually made me laugh. "Welcome to Bread Box, what can I get you?"

"I'll have the savory and sweet twelve pack, please."

"Anything else?" I knew that slightly unimpressed look wasn't reserved just for me, but it was fun to tease her.

"Two large black coffees and one latte, big as you have. What is it about me that you don't like Mara?"

She looked up at me, a hint of surprise in her eyes. "I don't know you to like you or not, Grant. But I don't mind looking at you, so there's that."

I laughed at her brutal honesty. "Thanks. I like looking at you too. A woman scowling at me every day keeps me humble."

"Humble? I'll believe that when I see it." She laughed as she turned away to prepare the coffees and I laughed again.

Maybe I wasn't exactly humble, but Brenna seemed to think so. As gorgeous as she looked in those tight jeans and bright red top, the most memorable part of the date had been her coming to my defense trying to prove I was as special as my brothers. It wasn't true, but I appreciated it anyway.

Ah, hell, I couldn't wait to see the woman again. She had

gotten under my skin and I liked spending time with her, with and without our clothes on.

"Ew, don't have dirty thoughts while you're in my line." Mara glared at me as she set the coffees on a tray and went to retrieve the pastries.

"You can't stop my thoughts, Mara. No matter how hard you scowl at me."

She laughed and it lit up her whole face. "My scowl might not be effective, but if I catch you having dirty thoughts about Brenna in front of me again, I'll put laxative in your favorite donuts."

I swallowed hard, knowing this woman wasn't one to bluff, but I couldn't resist. "You don't even know my favorite donut."

"Bavarian cream."

"Dammit. Fine, no more dirty thoughts."

Her smile brightened. "Have a wonderful day!"

"You're evil," I assured her with a shudder.

"Thanks for noticing. Later, Lopez."

The guys were in serious deep conversation when I got back to the table. "What did I miss?"

Liam groaned. "Miles called this meeting to con us into helping him plan his engagement party."

"For real, man? Again?"

Miles didn't look the least bit apologetic. "Yep. Look inside, I had Mara make mini breakfast burritos as a bribe."

As if we'd say no, after years of saving each other's asses both on and off the battlefield. "Works for me, I guess. Are strippers appropriate for engagement parties?"

Miles groaned and shook his head. "Maybe I should have just asked the Time for Love girls."

"It's not too late," Liam added while he double-fisted breakfast burritos.

It was the first time in my life I'd ever attended a meeting to plan a party, but that's what you did for friends who were like family. "It's Texas, how about a hoedown theme?"

Liam snorted. "Shannon is a city girl through and through, do black tie Texas." Miles and I both froze and turned to Liam. "What?"

"First of all," Miles began, "what the hell is black tie Texas?"

"And second," I added. "How do you even know how to put those words together?"

"Easy. I listen when my woman talks, you two should try it. Dicks."

"Listening, that's when her mouth is moving, right?" It was guaranteed to get a laugh, which it did. "Does that work naked too?"

"It does," Miles said easily. "How do you think I ended up planning this engagement party?"

Raucous laughter erupted all around the table, drawing smiles and stares from the rest of the bakery. I don't know how much party planning was done, but we had a good time and ate a lot.

I'd call that a win. My phone rang and I picked it up without looking, because Casper called when he had a spare moment, which was always at odd times. "Hello?"

The other end of the call was quiet but not silent, sounds of traffic came through but that was about it.

"Hello? Is anybody there?"

More silence.

"Cool," I said sarcastically. "Good talk, asshole." The guys stared at me and I shrugged. "Wrong number. Or someone chickened out of dirty talk." I wondered for a brief moment, if it was Brenna, but I shook it off when a quick look at the screen said the call was from a blocked number.

"A bitter ex?" Liam smiled, brows arched knowingly.

"My women are never bitter," I assured him confidently.

"Except the ones who want more than you're willing to give," Miles shot back quickly. Too quickly, if you asked me.

"They know the score." I always made sure the women knew, up front, that I was a loyal and honest guy, but I wasn't a forever guy.

"I'm not sure you know the score," Liam said, his expression suddenly dark. "Guys looking to have fun don't generally use a matchmaker."

"Now you sound like my mom."

"She's a smart woman. Tell her I said so, maybe I'll get some of those barbecue enchiladas."

"Or the huevos rancheros grilled cheese," Miles added excitedly. My mom tried to make up for my dad's long absences overseas by creating recipes she thought blended her Mississippi heritage with his Mexican heritage. The results were always a treat. "Hey, your mom is totally invited to the engagement party, Grant. Food is always a welcome gift."

"No way, she might start getting ideas, and I'm not ready to break her heart yet."

Her greatest disappointment in life was that none of her sons were married, depriving her of the daughters she'd always wanted, and the grandchildren she couldn't wait to spoil.

CHAPTER 7
BRENNA

"You're really going to let Miles plan the engagement party? The whole thing?" I sent Shannon a skeptical look through the mirror while I wiped down the flat surfaces in the salon. She'd stopped by for a last-minute trim and stayed for girl talk, something I hadn't had enough of lately.

Shannon nodded, one hand palming her growing belly, a wide smile illuminated her natural beauty. "Yep. He says he wants to do it and he's been asking for my input every step of the way, but between the bakery and getting things ready for the baby, I find that I don't mind handing over the reins."

"But this is a party, honey, and you're so…elegant. Aren't you worried it'll end up being a backyard barbecue or military theme party?"

She barked out a laugh. "A little bit, but it's his party too, and if that's what he wants, then I'm all right with it." She let out another, smaller laugh. "At least that's what I'm saying now. With these hormones, I might have the whole thing planned by this time tomorrow."

"I've never been engaged before, but I'm good with details, so if you or Miles need any help, you know where to find me. Here. Always here." I worked too much, but it was exciting to have my own salon, especially one that thrived.

"Not always," she said in a knowing tone. "You've been spending some time with Grant, I hear."

"You hear? I told you all about the sushi date." The good and the bad, and I even shared the details of that kiss that knocked me for a loop.

"But you haven't really given me any details about you and Grant. Are you guys dating now? Just screwing? Getting serious?"

"That's because I don't have any details. The dates have been fun, but two dates in two weeks isn't exactly dating-dating, is it?" I'd seen sex buddies more often than that in the past. "I think we're friends with occasional benefits."

"Yeah right. You forgot that I was there when you met. I saw the sparks with my own eyes. Felt the chemistry, too."

"That was months ago. This is now and things have changed." When we were together it didn't feel that way, but there was so much distance and silence between the dates that I was fairly sure we were both just staving off boredom and loneliness.

"I don't believe that any more than you do."

"Oh, I believe it." I had no choice to but take Grant by his actions, which said he liked spending time with me, but he wasn't looking for more than an occasional companion. "I'm done seeing signs where none exist, and reading between the lines when a man's words are explicit. That's old Brenna. New Brenna is much smarter."

"And incredibly oblivious," Shannon said and pointed to the street, where a uniformed delivery driver headed straight for the salon, a bouquet of flowers nestled in the crook of his arms. "So, so oblivious."

"It's probably from Jessie May because I told her how well the salon was doing." Besides Jessie May, the only time I ever got flowers was when my man of the moment screwed up, which was often. And that made the flowers feel a lot less special, almost tainted.

"Your sister sends you pink and white roses?"

I gasped and turned back just as the bell chimed to signal someone had entered the shop, and sure enough, the man held a gorgeous bouquet of pink and white roses and tulips. "They're beautiful!" I accepted the flowers and buried my face in them to inhale the sweet perfume.

"Read the card." Shannon's sing-song words drew my attention to the small envelope attached to the center of the bouquet.

"It's from Grant."

"Duh," she said sarcastically. "Read it. Out loud," she added with a laugh.

The card was handwritten. "I know last-minute requests break some unwritten date rules, but I wasn't sure I'd be free in time. Now that I know I will, I find that I can't wait to see you again. I'm so eager to see you that I'm luring you with a home cooked meal made by yours truly. Eight o'clock." I looked up with an unstoppable smile. "And his name. That's it."

"He wants to cook you dinner and probably eat you up

for dessert. Sounds like a good night to me. You're going right?"

"Yep. I can't resist a man who cooks," I told her honestly. "At least I think I can't, but I've never had a man who cooked for me before."

"Then enjoy every moment of tonight. And be sure to stop in at the bakery to share every single detail with me tomorrow." Shannon pushed off the chair with one hand on her belly. "See you later, Bren."

After I finished up at the salon, I made a quick stop home for a shower and a change, putting on a sexy floral dress that showed off all my curves, feminine open-toe wedge sandals, and knock'em dead lingerie just in case Grant was ready to fulfill his promise of more naked time. A quick spritz of perfume and I jumped in my small pink pickup truck and headed to Grant's place, which used to be Miles' lake house before he moved in with Shannon.

"Damn Brenna, you trying to give me a heart attack?"

"I was hopin' to get a rise out of you, but in an entirely different way."

The smile came first and then that deep, contagious laugh echoed in the open doorway. "You never fail to get a rise out of me, Brenna. Of that I can assure you. Come on in."

"You all settled in now?"

He shrugged and turned with a bemused smile. "I'm still getting used to the way news travels in this town, but yeah, I'm pretty much settled in."

The place looked every inch the bachelor pad it was, only it was sparser than I'd expected from a man who led such a rich life and seemed to make friends wherever he went. "Where are all the photos and other mementos?"

"In a box somewhere, I think. I don't know where to put crap like that," he admitted with a frustrated groan.

"Your business partners are both either married, or practically married, ask Shannon or Olive to help." Or me, but I didn't say that because it felt too much like I was inviting myself over again, which I was not. Absolutely not.

"Yeah I thought about that but they might put doilies up everywhere."

"Oh the horror," I deadpanned.

"Right?" He flashed a playful grin and tugged me into the kitchen where he wrapped his arms around me and greeted me with a proper kiss that turned my legs into limp spaghetti.

"It smells good in here, and it's not just you." Even though he smelled incredible, like fresh shower, man and a hint of something I identified as uniquely Grant.

His arms squeezed a little tighter before he released me. "I've got steaks and potatoes on the grill, and a salad because I know women love to nibble on rabbit food."

I laughed. "I thought we already covered that I rarely eat raw vegetables, even though they are excellent for clear skin."

"And you do have beautiful skin," he growled and buried his face in my neck. The next thing I felt was his lips dotting kisses along my exposed collarbone. "And you smell good too."

"The better to lure you in," I purred in his ear.

The timer on his phone sounded and Grant pulled back with a reluctant groan. "Gotta check the meat. You want beer or whiskey? I forgot to pick up wine on the way home."

"Too excited for dinner?"

"Something like that," he replied with a crooked, sheepish groan.

"Whiskey sounds nice. But only one, since I do have to drive home later." Much later, I hoped.

"We'll see about that," he said, erotic intent burning up his green eyes until they were so dark the color was indiscernible. "Come on, let's enjoy the last of the sunshine over the lake."

That sounded suitably romantic, but I quickly shook that thought off and decided to just enjoy each moment for what it was, an enjoyable moment with a delicious man. "This is one spectacular view."

"Not as good as looking at you, but yeah, I like it." His lips quirked up on one side into one of those sexy, lazy grins, the kind that pulled you right back into bed even though you had to get to work five minutes ago.

"Oh, you're good. Really good."

"Just because it sounds like a line, doesn't mean it *is* a line." I gave him a questioning look and Grant laughed. "Okay, technically it is a line, but it also happens to be the truth. You look gorgeous tonight, Brenna. Floral looks good on you."

I was moments away from shimmying right out of my dress and begging him to take me, right there on the deck overlooking the lake. Thankfully another timer sounded, saving me from myself.

"Looks like dinner is ready, which is perfect, because I was promised a home cooked meal."

He stood a little taller, his chest and shoulders almost seemed to expand a little as he did so. "And I am a man who doesn't break his promises. "Have a seat and I'll be back soon."

A few minutes later, Grant rejoined me on the patio wearing an apron that said "kiss the cook" as he set the table, adding a single sunflower to a small vase, and one fat candle for ambiance. "Wow, you're going all out. Be careful or I just might start to feel special, Grant."

"As far as I can tell, you are special Brenna."

"Me?" I casually brushed off his words. "Nah, I'm pretty normal."

"No you're not," he laughed. "Normal is predictable, some might even say boring, and you are none of those things Brenna. None at all."

I liked to think that was the case, but it was nice to hear someone else say it and mean it as a compliment. "Neither is this steak," I told him, unsure where to take the conversation because, apparently, my flirting skills were a little rusty.

"Thanks. I'm glad you like my meat."

I nearly choked on my food. "You did not just say that." It was such a childish thing to say, so unexpected that it teased a laugh from me, and not one of those third date laughs that was mostly fake, it was an honest to goodness body shaking laugh. "Yes Grant, I find your meat quite...impressive."

"Thanks. I marinated it myself."

It really was a juicy piece of meat, but talking about his meat for another second felt like, I don't know, temptin' fate or something. "Did you learn to cook from your momma, or in the Navy?"

"My dad, actually. When he was home, he did most of the cooking and he was patient about teaching. My mom is a damn fine cook, but she just grabs a bunch of ingredients, puts it all together and magic happens. So far that hasn't worked for me."

"You get the Lopez from your momma or your daddy?"

His lips pulled into a grin. "You nervous?"

"Not at all. Just curious about you, that's all."

His expression said, *okay, I'll play*, but his eyes sparkled with mischief and amusement. "My dad is the Lopez, but I mostly take after my mother."

"Even the dimple?"

Grant smiled. "Yeah. Mom has them on both cheeks and she thinks they make her look like a little girl."

"Bet she appreciates that youthfulness now."

"She does," he said with a hint of surprise in his voice. "Any other questions?"

"Just one. What's for dessert?"

Grant laughed. "You are, of course." Heat suffused my whole body and a titter of laughter escaped. "Too much?"

I shook my head. "I'll let you know if it becomes too much."

Grant stood and held his hand out to me. "You mean when, you'll let me know *when* it becomes too much." Then he pulled me close until I was flush up against his body and smiled before his lips came down on mine. There was no build up with this kiss though. It started hot as hell and it only got hotter with every swipe of his tongue, every journey his big strong hands made up and down the length of my back.

I groaned and he swallowed it and pressed his body even closer to mine, close enough that I could feel how hard he was, how hungry he was for me. I smiled because we were on the same page and I let my hands roam the wide expanse of his back and his chest, down the hard planes of his back to his tight ass. Then my hands found the button of his jeans. His zipper.

Suddenly my feet were in the air and Grant was carrying me inside the house, his mouth still on mine. We made it through the kitchen, but he stopped in the hallway just before the living room and pulled back with a smile. "I want you, Brenna."

"I'm right here, Grant." I licked my lips and smiled. "Have me."

That's just what he did, right there up against the wall, Grant slid deep, his strong legs holding up the weight of us both of us, his hips pumping hard and fast into me while we panted our pleasure. The sounds of our desire blended with the crickets and river outside.

His body was so hard and so strong I could hardly catch my breath. "Grant," I moaned when his lips left mine, giving me a chance to catch my breath even as he pumped his pleasure into my body while his lips tracked across my collarbone, up my throat so he could nibble my chin and my jawline. It was an onslaught of pleasure I couldn't have imagined, and all I could do was hold on tight as my orgasm barreled out of me, his name a song on my lips.

"Damn, Brenna. I'm not sure I'm gonna be able to get enough of you."

I ignored the way those words caused a hitch in my chest and nibbled his earlobe. "You'll have to," I whispered as I slid down the length of his body until my wedges hit the floor. "Because as soon as my legs work again, I need to get home."

His shoulders fell, but there was still a determined glint in his eyes as he scooped me in his arms and carried me down the hall to his spacious, masculine bedroom, decorated in shades of brown and gold. "Then I guess I'll have to do something about those legs, won't I?"

He set me on my feet and stared at me with heat in his glazed eyes as I unzipped my dress and stepped out of it, leaving me in nothing but the red lacy lingerie. "I'm willing to let you try."

He did more than try, giving me enough orgasms to stock up for winter, and guaranteeing that I couldn't walk properly to my car just before the sun came up.

CHAPTER 8
GRANT

I woke up the morning after another great date with Brenna with a little bit of residual electricity coursing through my veins. The sun was shining bright, a perfect match to my mood. I didn't even let myself get frustrated when I received two hang up calls before I got to the office, just grabbed my coffee mug and headed inside the Security Training Academy building.

"Grant, there you are. Get in here." He waved me inside his office like there was some big secret. I found Liam was already in there and he was wearing his end of the day annoyed expression. "I need your help. Both of you."

"More engagement crap?" I had no problem with the notion of love, but holy hell this party was already getting on my nerves. "What now?"

"Shannon loved the black-tie Texas idea, and I was up half the night trying to figure out what the hell that meant."

I laughed and smacked a hand on his desk as I sat. "And what the hell does it mean?"

"Fancy clothes with cowboy boots and hats. Bolo ties. Upscale barbecue. Stuff like that." He raked a hand through his hair and let out an exhausted breath. "I just need a little bit of help."

Liam and I looked at each other, silently deciding how much longer we should give Miles shit before we agreed to help. Liam shrugged and I rolled my eyes. "Fine. What do you need that has nothing to do with flowers or decorations?" That wasn't my area of expertise, and I had no desire to become a flower expert.

"Booze," he said with a relieved smile. "I need you to drive to the liquor depot in Tulip and pick up the order."

That was easy. "No problem."

"And put the deposit down for the lawn furniture. That's it. I swear."

"For now," Liam mumbled under his breath. "I'm not doing this again for your damn baby shower or whatever."

Baby shower? I jumped from my seat. "Oh, look at the time. First class starts soon. Gotta go. See you later." Baby talk was worse than wedding talk in terms of topics I had no desire to talk about.

"Oh look at Grant, running away," Miles laughed. "I can't wait until he falls. It's gonna be so satisfying."

Liam let out a loud bark of laughter. "He'll fight it so hard, thinking he can stop it from happening. I tried that. Didn't work."

"I can still hear you guys."

Liam looked back with a fake look of surprise. "You're still here? Weird. I thought the baby talk might have scared you off."

"I don't scare easily." They were screwing with me and I knew it, but still I couldn't let the ribbing go silently.

"I don't know," Miles added with a teasing smile. "You sure shot out of that chair like someone lit your ass on fire. It's okay, we're all scared of love and babies…until it happens to us."

"I'm not scared, I just don't do that." I had no problem with other people falling in love and succumbing to the trap of marriage and parenthood, but it wasn't my jam.

"When you find the right woman, you won't see it that way." Liam shook his head. "You think I planned on being a father? Hell no, but fate took it out of my hands and put the woman I was supposed to be with right in front of me, in a way that was impossible to ignore."

Hearing Liam talk so openly about his feeling and his relationship with Olive took me back. I didn't doubt his love for her, but fate? That was unexpected. "You really believe in fate?"

"I didn't at first. But falling for the woman I'd gotten pregnant during a one night stand, can't ignore signs like that. None of us can."

"Luckily I don't have to worry about that because I wrap it up. Always." It was a point of pride with me, that I never let myself get so wrapped up in the moment that I accidentally attach myself to a woman for the rest of my life.

"Yeah, because accidents don't happen." Miles shook his head and pointed between himself and Liam. "Look at us as perfect examples, Grant. Ninety-nine point nine ain't one hundred. That's all I'm saying."

"All right, fine. Then let's just say my luck hasn't run out."

"Yet," my so called best friends said at the exact same time, with entirely too much amusement.

"You never know," Miles said with a shrug. "Maybe Brenna is that woman for you. I was there for your first meeting, remember?"

How could I forget? The woman was such a spitfire, I wanted to take her home right then and there. But she shot me down. Hard. "I remember. It's just chemistry."

"That's how it starts. Fucking chemistry," Liam grumbled with a smile on his face. "Next thing you know, you're married and painting a second nursery. It's exhausting and amazing, but maybe you don't want all that."

He was taunting me, I knew that, but a small part of me could admit to a certain amount of envy that Miles and Liam seemed so damn happy. They were settling down and having enough babies to populate our own Navy someday, but I couldn't deny they seemed happy. Really, really happy.

"You guys in the matchmaking business now?"

"Nope," Liam said as he stood and clapped his hands together. "Just trying to help you avoid the same mistakes that almost cost us our women. Do what you want." With those parting words, Liam ambled out of Miles' office, but I was pretty sure I heard a muttered, "Idiot," before he disappeared down the hall.

"He's got no tact, but Liam's not wrong. Don't run because you're used to running, Grant. That's all. Oh, and don't forget the booze. I'll email you the address and order form. Thanks."

"Right." After all this talk of love and family, I was ready to burn off the nervous energy and I had just the way to do it. Our newest class of security trainees had arrived this morning and I was the first to get my hands on them. I found the group of elite retired military officers from all branches, and I had a brand new course designed to push them to their limits.

"All right men, who's ready to sweat?" This was my favorite part of the business. Sure, the corporate clients were great and provided an obscene amount of revenue, but training these guys, this was where I thrived. They all knew how quickly any scenario could become life and death, and the only way to cure that was to be prepared. For anything. "I said, who's ready?"

Loud whistles and applause went up and I grinned. Enthusiasm was another key factor and I didn't let my guys get away with half-assing their training. It was physically and mentally grueling, and by the end of the day I was just as exhausted as they were, but it was that happy, almost rewarding kind of exhaustion that meant sleep was hours away.

And since I was recharged and wide awake, there was just one place I wanted to be. The Big Tease.

CHAPTER 9
BRENNA

"All right now, Shirl. I'm gonna need you to promise me that you won't get it in your head ever again to do this on your own." Shirl was another of my elderly regulars, and she was an old school southern belle who believed in getting a cut and curl every other week. She didn't even check her mail unless she wore full makeup and a nice outfit. She opened her mouth to give another excuse and I aimed a long, hot pink nail at her. "If you can't afford it, come to me and we'll work something out. I heard you make a killer enchilada pie."

That took all the wind out of the old woman. "The trick is jalapeno and adobo peppers. Plus ketchup, but that's our little secret."

I nodded, unable to stop the smile that spread across my face at this stubborn woman. She'd come into the shop almost two hours ago, head looking like a blueberry. Now it was closer to lavender, which I was taking as a win.

"Your secret is safe with me, as long as I have your word

than you'll leave the dye jobs up to me. Because I can't have people thinking I did that to your hair!"

Shirl nodded with a sheepish smile and she reached out her soft wrinkled hand to pat my cheek. "You're such a good girl, Brenna. I hope you can make it work with that handsome military boy. He's big and strong and gorgeous, just what a girl like you needs."

"A woman doesn't need a man, Shirl. She has one because she wants him."

She rolled her brown eyes skyward. "That's what you say now, but every day I wake up without my Harold, it sure as heck feels like I need him. But I'm an old lady, what do I know?" She laughed and slowly pushed herself out of the salon chair.

"You don't know how to dye your hair," I called after her.

"Funny and pretty? He'd be lucky to keep you, honey!"

I shook my head at yet another matchmaking senior, there was a surplus of them in Pilgrim, it seemed, always ready to offer you advice on everything from fashion choices to modern relationships. Shirl shuffled towards the door, gasping in surprise when she found Grant holding it open for her with his most charming smile.

"Looking good, Shirl. Purple is definitely your color."

She put a hand to her hair, pleased as punch at his compliment. "Well, thanks. Brenna fixed me right up."

"Now don't go givin' the old guys heart problems with this new look, you hear?" She tittered and Grant laughed with her. "Have a good evening, Shirl."

"You too, boy. You too." He was such a flirt, even Shirl wasn't immune to his charms.

Grant watched her walk off down the street and I noticed the old girl had a little extra bounce in her step. When he turned that killer, smiling gaze my way, I took a deep breath. He really was too damn handsome for a woman to think straight, and I needed to think straight around this man.

"Brenna."

"Grant," I said in the most neutral voice I could muster, which was hard when he stood there staring at me like it was his first time seeing me. "This is a surprise. You here for a trim?"

His smile widened as one big hand slid through his thick brown waves. "Sure. Why not?"

"Have a seat," I told him and busied myself with organizing everything I needed for a quick cut. "How was your day?" It was a stylist's favorite question, because those four little words allowed the person in the chair to carry on until the job was done.

"Good. Exhausting with the new class of trainees. How about your day? Did you make the whole town beautiful?"

"I did my part." It was nice to be around a man who didn't belittle my work, as if they didn't want us looking our absolute best twenty-four-seven. "They all come in here beautiful, I just highlight it for them."

He laughed. "You do more than that, but I'm finding your modesty as appealing as your blunt honesty." Truth and heat sparkled in his eyes.

"Did you reach your goal yet, of charming the whole town?"

"Not yet," he said and held up two sets of crossed fingers. "Any day now, though, I'm sure."

"You're a determined guy, I'm sure you'll reach your goal sooner rather than later."

Grant let out an adorable snort of laughter, and even though I was focused on his hair, I felt the weight of his stare through the mirror. "You want to ride with me to Tulip tomorrow? I promised Miles I'd get the alcohol for his engagement party, and I figured we could enjoy the best pizza in Texas, according to my friend Reese."

"Does your *friend* Reese happen to work at this pizza restaurant?"

He barked out another utterly masculine laugh. "No, but I appreciate the jealousy. Reese owns a barbecue restaurant, which is damn good, but she swears this pizza is worth the drive."

"Since you're driving, I have a feeling she's right. So yeah, I'll give you a few hours of my time tomorrow night." Spending time with this man was starting to be one of my favorite past times.

Right now, though, being this close to him was pure torture. He was freshly showered, smelling like man and ocean with maybe just a hint of leather. "You smell good." I hadn't meant for the words to slip out, but that's what happened when you were in a constant state of arousal.

"Thanks. Just my natural aroma."

I smacked his arm. "You wish."

"I wish for lots of things, Brenna. For example, I spent most of the day wishing for one of your sweet kisses."

Me too. They were more intoxicating than my granddaddy's moonshine, and I was slowly becoming an addict. "So you showed up for a cut and a kiss?"

"Nah, the cut was just so I could get nice and close to

you." His arms snaked around my waist and Grant pulled me close.

When our lips touched, I felt it all the way down to my bones. We stood there and kissed like we were completely alone in the world, like two lovers who'd been separated across the decades, like two people who couldn't get enough of each other. But we weren't alone and worse than that, The Big Tease was public. Very, very public. I pulled back and nodded at the big picture windows. "The whole town can see us. Wouldn't want to ruin your reputation."

Grant though, was completely nonplussed by my words and pulled me closer until I dropped down in his lap with a squeal. "I have no reputation, and who better to ruin it with? Now come here woman and let me finish that kiss." It was long and hot and shot straight through to the heart of me. My core and my skin, pebbled with goosebumps brought on by the touch of his roughened skin against mine.

It was a kiss that begged for more, which I would have happily given, in another time and place. I pulled back, breathless and smiling. "What was that for?"

"I told you, been thinking about tasting those sweet lips all damn day. Is that okay with you?"

I nodded. It was more than okay. "Hell yeah. It was a good kiss. A hot kiss."

"Perfect." He gave my ass a little smack. "Now get back to my haircut, I'm taking a pretty girl to dinner tomorrow night and I want to impress her."

"It'll take more than a haircut to impress her," I shot back and reached for my spray bottle, comb and scissors. My body shook with desire while I gave the quickest haircut of my life and took a step back to examine him from all angles.

"All finished. I don't know if you'll impress her, but you sure do look pretty."

"Thanks. I picked these jeans out all by myself," he joked and followed me to the cash register, paying and tipping too much for the short trim. "You hungry, Brenna?" He asked the question as if he didn't know that I was absolutely ravenous for nothing but him.

"Sure am," I said casually.

He flashed a wide grin and leaned across the small counter until our lips were less than a breath apart. "Meet at your place in twenty?"

Hell yes. "I think I can pencil you in."

"I'll see you in twenty."

I let out a shuddery breath and nodded, thinking about how much a woman could accomplish in twenty minutes with the right motivation. The answer came quickly because the man standing in front of me was more than six feet of motivation.

"I'll be waiting."

CHAPTER 10
GRANT

The drive to Tulip was mostly quiet, dead silent actually. I didn't know what was on Brenna's mind, but my thoughts were full of her from last night. Deceptively innocent pink and white lingerie, pale skin and rosy nipples peeking through the lacy material. Lush pink lips formed into a perfect pout when she answered the door. It was hot as hell, as was everything that came next, and it all played on a permanent reel in my mind.

Non-fucking-stop.

She let out a shuddery breath beside me and my cock hardened, returning me to last night with those big blue eyes staring up at me while she took me in her mouth, keeping me hot and hard until she drove me out of my mind. Completely. Totally. Last night was even hotter than the first night, and I spent all day at the office daydreaming about all the ways I'd had her. Up against the door. Spread across the sofa. The kitchen table. The bedroom. And finally, the shower. The guys gave me shit about my spaced out look all day and I didn't care, I took it all because I couldn't get the image of her out of my mind.

"Is everything all right, Grant?" Her sweet voice, clear and crisp with that twang, brought me back to the here and now.

I risked a quick glance and frowned. "What?"

"You're awful quiet and I'm wonderin' if you're all right. Bad day at work?"

I smiled in response to her concern and nodded. "I'm good, Brenna. Really good, actually. A little distracted though."

"Yeah?" Her red lips curled into a grin. "By anything in particular?"

"Oh yeah. This beautiful woman I saw last night, she's got my head all mixed up so that all I can think about is her."

A sexy little blush stained her cheeks and Brenna sat up a little taller, her smile a bit bigger. "Last night was pretty great, wasn't it?"

"Better than great, sweetheart. It was unforgettable. Truly." We shared a quick smile before I turned back to the road as we entered the town of Tulip, as small and idyllic as Pilgrim, but with a more storied beginning. "You know about Tulip?"

Brenna huffed out a laugh. "The badass woman who bucked tradition by refusing to marry a very rich but terribly old man, and turned around to found a town? Yeah, I know all about this place. What a testament to female strength, don't you think?"

"Hell yeah. I can't help but admire people who make their own way in the world. Strong women are a real turn on for me."

She laughed and stepped from the car—without waiting for me—when we got to the liquor depot. "I imagined you were surrounded by strong women in the military. That couldn't have been comfortable, being turned on all the time."

I laughed and held the door open so she could enter first. "No. The women were strong as hell, but they were teammates, they were part of the unit. One of the guys, no matter how pretty." I wasn't one of those guys who could hit on anything with tits, especially in a warzone.

"Look at you, being all forward thinking. Now *that* is a real turn on, Grant."

"Good to know," I whispered in her ear, smiling at the shiver produced by my closeness. "Come on, let's take care of this order so we can get some grub." It didn't take much time since Miles had already placed the order and paid for it.

"Is that everything?" The woman behind the counter looked at the receipt and then to me.

"Uh, yeah. That's what's in the order, right?" This wasn't my party, I was merely the delivery man. "Right?"

"There's no champagne?" That question came from Brenna with an accompanying frown.

"Miles didn't say anything about champagne."

"But it's an engagement party, where you're celebrating the fact that two people are about to combine their lives."

I snorted. "Right, but Shannon can't drink."

"But the rest of us can toast her, Grant." Her words were

even and calm, but there was an underlying hint of her thinking I was an idiot. "Or, this is fine."

I groaned. "Can you add a case of champagne to the order? I'll pay for it," I said and pulled out my wallet. "This will be my gift for the happy couple."

"I'm sure Shannon will appreciate it." I pretended to ignore the smile that she couldn't hide, or the pride that I'd done the right thing. "You're a good friend, Grant."

"Yeah, I'm a real saint. A saint really in need of pizza."

Brenna's laugh echoed down the aisles as we left the liquor depot. "Who knew you had such a pizza craving? I guess with a box of meat and cheese pizza, a person could easily lure you into their perv van."

I barked out a laugh and slid behind the wheel. "What the hell is a perv van?"

"You know, a van driven by a pervert who wants to lure you inside to do wicked things to you? They don't have those in Boston?" Her lips twitched before the teasing smile won the battle and lit up her face.

"No, they don't have them in Everett, either, which is where I actually grew up."

Her blue eyes lit up. "You're a small town kid too? I never woulda guessed!"

"It's not Tulip or Pilgrim small, but compared to Boston, yeah it's small." It as a nice suburban town, a good place to raise a family and make stupid mistakes that wouldn't haunt the rest of your life. "I don't recall any perv vans, though."

"There's a first time for everything," she said as her lips curled into a teasing grin. "If you're lucky."

"I'm always lucky, Brenna. It's my middle name." The

shocked look on her face was the last thing I saw as I stepped out of the car and jogged around to open her door. She beat me to it, once again.

"It is not!" She gave my shoulder a shove and I took advantage of her proximity and wrapped an arm around her waist, pulling her body flush up against mine.

"It is. Grant Lucky Lopez."

Her mouth dropped into a sexy, surprised 'O' and I couldn't resist one little kiss, right there under the golden glow of the pizza place parking lot. Her lips were sweet and pliable, a hint of a cherry taste. "Is Lucky trying to get lucky?"

"I got you here with me, don't I? I'm already lucky."

She rolled her eyes. "Cheesy, but I'll allow it because you're just so cute." Brenna turned away and I watched her hips swing left to right before I jogged to catch up with her.

"Cute? Puppies and kittens are cute. Child actors are cute. I'm handsome."

She laughed again. "Too damn handsome, if you ask me." Her phone buzzed inside her tiny purse and Brenna looked at the phone and dropped it back inside.

"Or, I'm just the right amount of handsome?"

"Let's go with that, but only because we're about to enjoy some of the best pizza in Texas. Allegedly."

"Hold your judgment until you've eaten."

Her phone buzzed again and she tapped the ignore button this time. "I'm not picky about toppings, but I do like bell peppers and spicy peppers on pizza."

"I can do that. And meat? How do you feel about meat on pizza, Brenna?"

"Chicken and bacon?"

"Ground beef and bacon," I shot back with a smile.

"Deal." She held out a hand for a shake, and I pulled it close to brush a kiss across her knuckles. Her phone rang again and after a quick glance, Brenna groaned. "Sorry. I better answer it now or Jessie May will just keep calling."

"I'll go place our order." I winked and stood, then turned to her with a smile. "It's okay if you stare at my ass while I walk away. I'd do the same to you."

She rolled her eyes, but the laugh she let out was throaty and sexy, enough to draw stares from two tables filled with appreciative men. "If you're still here, I can't stare, can I?"

Damn, this woman was hotter than lava, and my cock sprang to life once again as I walked away, thinking of pizza toppings to get my body under control. I stood behind a handsy older couple for a couple minutes before I placed our order and when I got back to the table, Brenna was still on the phone with her sister.

"That's great news, Jessie May. I'm so happy for you, both of you." Her twang was somehow thicker when she spoke to her sister. "Yeah, here he is." She turned the phone towards me and I gave a wary wave.

"Hello, sister Jessie May. How's it goin'?"

Jessie May gasped, studying me, which gave me plenty of time to notice the differences between the sisters. She was a blond too, but a natural dirty blond with light brown eyes and freckles on the bridge of her nose. Whereas Brenna looked like a country bombshell, her sister was the proverbial girl next door. "My, aren't you a handsome devil!" She clapped her hands and threw her head back with a laugh. "You didn't say he was *that* handsome, Bren!"

"Um, thanks?" I wasn't shy about my looks, but it had been a long time since a woman was so blatant in her appreciation.

"Are you married, Grant?"

I blinked, stunned by her question. "No ma'am, I'm not."

"Ever been married?"

"No, again." I scratched my head trying to figure out where this conversation was going.

"Good. How about kids, do you have any?"

I looked to Brenna who just shrugged. "No. I don't have any kids."

Brenna laughed. "Don't mind Jessie, she's pregnant again and has babies on the brain."

Oh. Good. My shoulders relaxed and I smiled at the woman staring back at me on the screen. "Congratulations on the new addition to your family."

"Thanks. Good looking *and* he's got good manners? This is definitely an improvement, Brenna. Definitely."

Brenna groaned and snatched the phone from my hand. "You've seen him and grilled him, now it's time for you to go."

"But, I haven't even asked-,"

"You shouldn't have wasted your questions, smarty pants. Our pizza is here so, gotta go!" She waved with one hand, her thumb stretching to surreptitiously ending the call. "Sorry about that but it had to be done."

"It did?"

She nodded. "Otherwise her curiosity would have her calling all night. Now she's laid eyes on you and talked to you, that's enough."

I blinked, surprised her sister knew anything about me. "You told her about me?"

"Sure did. There are no secrets between Jessie May and me. She knows we went out and had a good time. A few good times, which was giving her *ideas*." I swallowed, wondering if it was also starting to give Brenna *ideas*. I hoped not, because things were perfect just as they were. "I knew your face would distract her from talk like that."

"And it worked, on account of me being so outrageously good looking."

Brenna froze and then dropped her head backwards as a loud, husky laugh erupted out of her, causing more heads to turn. The young waitress wore a wide smile as she delivered our food, taking in the beautiful spectacle Brenna made, laughing at my expense. "Enjoy your meal."

The waitress startled Brenna, which produced another laugh. "My goodness you move like a ninja! I didn't even hear you come up on us." This time the young girl joined in, seemingly happier just being around the ray of sunshine that was Brenna McKenna.

"Sorry?"

"Oh, don't be honey. It was a good laugh and that never requires an apology. Thanks for the food."

"Enjoy your meal." She walked away with a smile that was much brighter than the professional one she wore when she arrived with the food.

"What?" Brenna blinked innocently and looked over one shoulder and then the other. "Why are you staring? And don't say I have food in my teeth because I haven't eaten a thing. Yet."

"Just watching. You have this effect on people, you know that right?"

She waved my words away and dropped a slice on my plate and then hers. "It's just my laugh. I've been told it's contagious."

It was more than that, but I could see it was useless to argue, and the steaming slice on my plate was calling my name. I plowed through four slices in the time it took Brenna to eat two. And a half. "Want something else?"

"Yeah, I call dibs on two of the leftover slices. They'll make a perfect midnight snack." She licked her lips and in that moment, I was jealous of those leftover slices.

"I'll take the rest, then." She laughed and shook her head, digging in her purse for...something.

Brenna pulled out a five dollar bill and I frowned. "What?"

"What are you doing?"

"Since you were kind enough to pay for dinner, I thought I'd leave the tip. Is that a problem?" Her tone told me to tread carefully, but there was a part of me that hated the idea of her paying for any part of the dinner. "Is it?"

I leaned forward and flashed my most charming smile. "No ma'am, not at all."

"Good. I'm ready to head out when you are." Her smile never wavered and dammit, it *was* contagious. "Unless you want that chocolate fudge brownie pie?"

"Only if you let me eat it off your body."

She sucked in a breath, her blue eyes darkened and her pupils dilated as the smallest intake of breath sounded between us. "That's about all I'll let you do after all that pizza."

"Fine by me," I told her and pushed the inside door open just as my friend Reese entered with a dark-haired man I assumed to be her boyfriend. "Reese?"

She looked up and gasped. "Grant Lopez, you handsome son of a gun, what are you doing in Tulip?"

"Picking up booze for my friend's engagement party. Thought I'd stop to check out the best pizza in Texas."

"And? Did you love it?" She posed the question to Brenna who nodded furiously.

"It was delicious, even better than Pilgrim Pizza, and that's sayin' something. Thanks for the recommendation." She held up the red and white paper bag. "I got extra slices for later."

"They're good hot or cold," she advised with a curious smile. "I didn't know Grant was seeing anyone."

"He's not. I'm just using him for sex. Brenna McKenna, nice to meetcha!" She looked at the guy at Reese's side. "And this one belongs to you?"

Reese laughed, amused by Brenna's flamboyance. "Yes. This is my husband, Jackson Slater, Tulip's very best detective."

The man wrapped an affectionate arm around her and extended the other to Brenna and then to me. "Just Jackson will be fine. Tulip grapevine says that you run a bodyguard school. Do you do law enforcement too?"

"It's a training academy for private security, but we do offer training and team building events." I found a business card and handed it over. "Call and see if we can meet your needs."

Reese laughed. "Wow, you sound like a proper businessman. I'm impressed."

I stood a little taller and let out a chuckle. "Not just a pretty face, anymore. You should be very impressed."

"I should, shouldn't I?" She smirked and shook her head. "I'll have to see you in action before I make up my mind. I'm so hungry right now, I can't think straight."

Brenna laughed. "It was nice meetin' y'all. Enjoy the pizza!" I kept a hand on Brenna's back until we were at my car. "She was nice. Sassy. I think I like her."

"I figured you'd say that, once you stopped being jealous."

She sucked in an outraged breath. "I was *not* jealous. Merely curious."

"Whatever you need to tell yourself, Brenna."

She gave my chest a playful shrug and slipped into the passenger seat with a grin. "I think you want me to be jealous."

"I don't *want* it, but it's nice you to know you care." The last thing I heard was the sound of her laughter as I closed the door and walked around the car. Brenna's laugh wasn't just contagious, it was addictive. The more she used that husky laugh on me, the more I wanted to hear it. The more I needed to hear it, and I found myself doing things just to make her laugh.

"Should I be jealous of a married woman, Grant?"

"Reese? No way. She's a great girl, but she's not my type at all. You are."

"Good answer."

I turned to her and wiggled my eyebrows. "Thanks. Wanna make out?" I was joking, mostly, but then Brenna shocked me when she leaned in and brushed a soft kiss against my lips.

"Yeah, I do."

I found a spot shielded by some overgrown trees, turned off the lights and had a make out session that would've made my fifteen year old self green with envy.

CHAPTER II
BRENNA

"This would probably look fabulous on you, Brenna." Shannon held up a bright red dress that looked like it might my hug my extra curves a little too much, but holy hell, it was stunning. "It says blond bombshell better than anything we've looked at all day."

I sighed as I took in the lace back of the dress, and admired the just below the knee length with a nod. Shannon was right, it was a gorgeous dress and we had been shopping for hours already, all in search of something to wear for the upcoming engagement party.

"It's very pretty," I said finally. "But isn't red kind of tacky when you're not the guest of honor?"

"Not if the guest of honor say it's fine, and I do. Add this to your try pile, pitifully small as it is." Shannon rubbed her belly and shook her head, looking every bit the disappointment mother that she was soon to be. "Don't tell me you're one of those women who hates to shop?"

Her tone was so appalled I couldn't help but laugh. "No, it's not that. Nothing is tickling my fancy, that's all." I grabbed the red dress and hung it on the dressing room door I'd commandeered for myself. "It's your party, Shannon, we need to find you a dress first."

"Unless you have something really fancy coming on an airplane from California?" Mara stood between us, hands on her hips, an impatient look on her face. "Please don't say that you do."

"Okay. I won't," Shannon laughed and winked at me. "Of course, I don't. You think I'd be here on my swollen feet if I had a dress flying in? Get real." She moved to another rack and flashed a look at me over her shoulder. "I'll keep looking while you tell us what's going on with you and Grant."

That was inevitable, I knew that, but still it shocked me. "We're just hanging out, I guess."

Mara snorted. "What the hell does that mean? Do adults even hang out?"

"These adults do," I shot back. "And it means that we spend time together, we have really good sex, and that's about it." It was a twist on friends with benefits, I supposed, except there was a real friendship between us.

"Sounds like dating to me," Mara said in a sing-song voice.

"Me too," Shannon added with an apologetic smile.

"Maybe, but it's not like we're *really* dating. Like I said, just hanging out." At least I thought that's what we were doing, but now I'm not sure if Grant is sending mixed messages, which men have been known to do, or if I just want more from him than I'm allowing myself to admit. "I don't know. The first three weeks we had three dates, keeping it casual, right? Then he sent flowers. Then he just stopped by because he couldn't stop thinking about kissing me. Honestly, I have no clue what the hell we're doing."

"Well," Mara began and turned with a silver dress draped over her shoulder. "What do you want to happen?"

"I don't know, and that's the God's honest truth. The fact that I like him at all means there's some fatal flaw I haven't uncovered yet." And the bigger, more troublesome problem was that I was slowly approaching the point where it would be too late if and when I did uncover the flaw. "We have an unspoken agreement to just keep our distance. Now, back to shopping?"

"Fine by me," Shannon said. "I'm about ten minutes away from needing food, and I think my try on pile is big enough."

Thirty minutes later Shannon had a gorgeous purple dress, Mara a flowing black jumper, and me, a royal blue dress with a fitted bodice and a skirt perfect for dancing, wrapped up to take with us as we exited the store. "How about burgers?" Shannon pointed to the burger joint across the street and we made our way inside. Shannon inhaled deeply and grinned. "I see a cheeseburger in my immediate future."

"I guess that's one good thing about being pregnant," Mara laughed. "You can eat all day and blame the baby."

"It is one of many good things," Shannon assured her. "Just you wait."

Mara shook her head. "Xander and I have decided to

take our time. There's no need to rush into parenthood when we haven't had enough time together. Just us." She turned her curious gaze to me. "The question is, what is Brenna gonna do about her feelings for Grant?"

"Nope. That's not the question, because I'm not going to do anything. We're adults who date casually and it'll end when it stops working for us. No one has to get hurt."

"Unless one of you catches a case of the feelings," Shannon said from behind her menu. "Are you coming to the party together?"

"No. He hasn't asked, and I've made plans to go on my own."

"You're not seriously this delusional?" Mara shook her head. "He will ask, and you'll say yes."

"That," Shannon said and pointed to Mara. "And don't let him get away too easily with a last-minute invite."

"We're friends. Standard dating rules don't apply."

"Ha!" Mara shook her head, taking a break to place her order. "That's what he wants you to think so he can keep playing Last Minute Larry with you. It's crap, and you shouldn't allow it."

"It's not that deep, y'all." I was being careful by being distant and not too needy. "I'm happy when he comes around, but I'm not longing for him when he's not."

"Good," they said at the same time and laughed like schoolgirls while I placed my order.

Considering the dress I just bought, I opted for a salad. A steak salad, but still. "Thanks." I was just about to tell them that I was fully capable of handling Grant when my phone chimed on the table and Shannon reached for it before I could. "Hey!"

"It's Grant. Wants to know if he can *escort* you to the engagement party." She looked up with arched brows. "You know, the one that's just a few days away?"

"Just give me the dang phone." Shannon laughed and then slid it across the table with a shrug. I looked down at the message and replied. "Afraid I'll find someone better at the party if I don't let you take me?"

Immediately a few laughing emojis appeared while he typed. "As if there is anyone better."

"Arrogant, much?" I felt my lips spread into a big, goofy grin and I wasn't ashamed at all.

"She's a goner," Mara groaned.

"Not much, no," he shot back with a wink.

"You might be right," Shannon replied, her voice filled with worry. Unnecessary worry. "Just be careful, Brenna."

"Sure," I texted back before staring into Shannon's worried eyes. "I am being careful, I promise. I like Grant, he's gorgeous and charming and makes me laugh like no other man who isn't a professional comedian, but I'm under no illusions about who he is. At least, I don't think I am."

"Well, he is pretty, so I can see how hard it might be to resist him, and if the sex is as good as you say it is, I'm afraid you might be screwed. Literally and metaphorically."

"Thanks, Mara. You're a constant burst of sunshine."

"Right?" Her deadpan delivery had us all exploding into a fit of giggles. "I'm just being honest about your options. Either jump in and risk getting hurt, or run in the other direction and give up those delicious orgasms."

"They *are* delicious." I leaned forward, suddenly curious. "Is that what you did with Xander?"

She nodded. "After running for years, yes. Basically. Eventually."

Well, that was no help at all.

Distance. I needed to keep my distance, and I would, after the engagement party.

CHAPTER 12
GRANT

When Brenna opened the door and I got my first look of her in that sexy blue dress, it literally stole my breath. The top part hugged her curves, producing the perfect hourglass that made my fingers itch to touch her, but the bottom half was sexy and flowing, with a big split up one side. And instead of those strappy little dainty heels women often preferred, she had on white cowgirl boots.

"Damn woman, you look beautiful."

A small flush crawled from her chest up to cover her cheeks. "Why, thank you, Grant. You look pretty damn gorgeous yourself." Just to make her point, big blue eyes scanned the length of my body, she smiled and gave a short nod before she stepped back. "Come in, I'm almost ready."

"You look ready to me."

"That's because you don't have an eye for detail. My lips are bare." She smacked her lips together and my control snapped.

"Perfect." I wrapped an arm around her waist and pulled her close enough that I could see the different colors of blue that swirled in her eyes a moment before my lips crashed against hers. Though there was no lipstick on her lips, they tasted like cherries. Sweet, plump cherries. I ravaged her mouth for several long minutes, enjoying the feel of the soft fabric as my hands traced her curves. "Damn." I growled and pulled back.

Brenna laughed and shook her head. "You got that right. Now, let me fix my lips so we can get outta here." She winked and then sauntered off with an extra swing in her hips.

"I'll be waiting," I told her and adjusted the erection making the front of my pants tight. Very, very tight. My phone rang and it was another unknown number, but I picked it up anyway. "Hello?"

Nothing. Just background noise.

"Hello?" More silence met my greeting and I hung up, shoving the phone back in my pocket.

"Ready?" Brenna appeared with lush bright red lips and I had to resist the urge to mess it up with my lips.

"Yeah, let's get going before we never make it out of here."

"Ha! You think I took all this time getting ready to not be seen in my brand new dress? I don't think so, Grant."

"Ouch. I think my ego was just bruised."

"Impossible," she said with a teasing grin. "It's just a few blocks to Miles and Shannon's place, let's take advantage of the weather and walk."

Since she had on cowgirl boots, I shrugged my agreement and took her hand as we strolled down the block. "I like your boots."

"Thanks. They're one of my favorites." She did a little foot twirl to show off the boots, complete with decorative buckles, and laughed. "You clean up real nice, Grant."

"I do, don't I?" She laughed and gave my shoulder a bump. We kept up a steady chatter on the short walk over, and Brenna even managed to ignore another hang up call with little more than a quizzical look.

By the time we arrived at the party, the music was loud and the drinks were flowing. "Should we dance or drink first?"

"Drink. Definitely a drink. Or two."

"Fine. Let's get you some liquid courage before we hit the dance floor." She laughed and tugged me towards the tent covered bar area. "Shannon, you look beautiful!" Brenna wrapped her in a hug. "That dress looks even better under the natural light of the sun."

"Thanks." Shannon turned her green eyes on me. "And thank you for the champagne. It was a good call."

"Told ya," Brenna sang and grabbed two bottles of beer.

"No problem. Happy to help, and Brenna's right, you look beautiful."

She rolled her eyes. "I look big and pregnant, but I'll take the compliment in the spirit it was given." Shannon gave me a side hug and kissed my cheeks. "Have fun."

Both me and Brenna took those words to heart, enjoying a couple beers each in between tearing it up on the dance floor. She let me twirl her around, pressed chest to chest during the slow songs and tried to teach me to line dance during the fast ones.

"You're learnin', but you definitely ain't a southern boy."

I didn't care, as long as she let me hold her close for hours upon hours. "Maybe it's my teacher."

She sucked in a breath and smacked my arm. "You take that back! I'm an excellent dance teacher." She put a hand to her stomach and sighed. "And I'm hungry." Brenna marched towards the back steps that led inside the repainted Victorian and I laughed.

"The food is the other way." Another tent had been erected where the buffet offered up barbecue meats and sides to satisfy everyone's hunger.

"It's called washing your hands, animal."

I laughed and followed her inside, because the truth was I just couldn't get enough of Brenna. The whole afternoon was like one of those romance movie montages, lots of dancing and flirting and laughing, playing on a seemingly never ending loop. She made it easy to forget we were at an engagement party where everyone had marriage on the brain. This woman had an odd effect on me, being around her made me feel good, and not just aroused. Being around her was just plain fun and we always had a good time together. Best of all, she didn't pressure me about getting a drawer at my house or closet space, she didn't make plans for future holidays, or talk about couple-y things like shared vacations. It was perfect.

Absolutely perfect.

When I stepped up behind her, Brenna laughed. "So you do have some home trainin'?"

"Some, but not too much." I wrapped my arms around her from behind and rested my chin on her shoulder. "I just came to get close to you."

Brenna purred and leaned into me, letting me take the weight of her lush curves pressed against me. "You're sweet."

"And you taste even sweeter."

"Yeah?" She turned in my arms and pulled me closer. "Wanna bet?"

I nodded and a second later, my lips crashed over hers and then everything was perfect in the world. Just perfect as our lips collided and our tongues danced together, her fingers tangled in my hair as if trying to get closer to me. My hands roamed up and down the length of her hips and her waist, stopping to grip her ass for just a moment. I pressed my hips against hers and smiled at the way she gasped against my lips.

The sound of a throat clearing made us both freeze and then laugh before we separated. "Guess we got a little carried away," she said and looked at the person who'd entered the kitchen. "Sorry about that. You're new, are you a friend of Shannon's from California?"

The woman was petite with dark hair and even darker eyes, but the jeans and hoodie she wore made her look like a teenager. So did the scowl she wore.

"Who's Shannon?"

Her words, tinged with anger, sent my defenses up and I took a step between her and Brenna. "Can I help you?"

The woman looked down at her phone and then back up at me. "You're Grant Lucky Lopez?"

I nodded, feeling even more confused now. "Yeah, that's me. What do you need?"

"What do I...?" She cut off her own words and shook her head. "I've been trying to find you, to reach you for a while."

Suddenly it all made sense. "You're the one who's been calling and hanging up?" I snorted. "Doesn't seem like you were trying all that hard. What is it that you want from me?"

"Yeah well, this isn't the kind of news you deliver over the phone, especially since it took me two years to track you down." She shook her head, annoyed and pissed off. "This," she put her hand on the shoulder of a small girl with big brown eyes and dark brown hair, "is your daughter. Her name is Mariana."

I stared down at the little girl with an all too familiar dimple in her left cheek, her amber brown eyes stared up at me, filled with apprehension and sadness. "This can't be my child since I don't know you. Never met you."

She laughed and shook her head. "Mariana isn't my daughter, she's my goddaughter. Her mother was Alyssa Morgan. From Nashville."

Nashville. That was all I needed to hear to remember a blond with big brown eyes mixed with amber. We had a fun-filled week in music city about...shit, eight years ago. "Oh."

"Alyssa died two and a half years ago. Cancer. I'm her best friend, and I've been taking care of Mariana since she passed."

"Dead? She was so young." So vibrant.

"Yeah, it turns out cancer doesn't give a damn about any of that." She angrily swiped away a few tears and walked Mariana towards me. "Mariana needs a family, she needs her father, and since we've finally found you, she's yours now."

Mine. "Wait, what? I don't know anything about taking care of a little girl."

"Yeah well, neither did Alyssa and neither did I. We managed, and if you can manage in a war zone, you can manage a little girl." She smiled down at Mariana and then back at me. "Is there somewhere you and I can talk? Privately?"

Brenna squatted down to look at the sad little girl with a wide grin. "I can take Mariana outside if you'd like. There's barbecue and soda pop and a whole table filled with desserts." Her blue gaze darted between me and the angry woman for approval.

"It's all right," she finally said. "Go on, Mariana."

Brenna held out her hand patiently until the little girl took it, and guided her out of the kitchen and into the backyard. "Chocolate or sprinkles on your ice cream?"

"She's good with her. That should make this easy for you."

"Oh, we're not a couple," I insisted. "She's a friend."

"Right." She shrugged off a backpack and dropped it on the counter, rifling through it until she produced a folder packed with documents. "Legal documents, including Mariana's birth certificate which lists you as the father."

"That doesn't mean...never mind." I wasn't a jerk, and I remembered that Alyssa wasn't all that experienced in the world of casual sex. Besides all that, Mariana could be me or either of my brothers when we were kids. "I'm not ready for a child."

"Neither was Alyssa. You think single and abandoned was how she envisioned becoming a mother?"

"I didn't abandon her, I didn't know about the child."

"And you never called her again, did you?"

I didn't. "She knew my stay in Nashville was temporary.

I spent the ensuing three years on missions, but if she'd left a message it would have gotten to me, so don't lay your blame at my feet." I would take responsibility for a lot of things, but not for something I knew nothing about.

She sighed. "You're right. I tried to get her to look for you, to find you, but she didn't want to interrupt the *important work* you were doing. But Alyssa isn't here anymore, and she wanted you to have Mariana." She produced an envelope from the folder with my name on it. "She left you a letter. I'm going to say goodbye to Mariana, for now, and don't you even think of keeping me from her."

"You're family to her, then you're always welcome. I guess."

She let out a bitter laugh. "See? You're learning. Good luck, Grant Lucky Lopez."

"Hey. What's your name?"

"I'm Luna." Then she was gone and as I watched her slow, sluggish footsteps towards the little girl, I realized how hard this was for her too.

Inevitably I thought of how significantly my life had just changed. A father. In charge of a child, responsible for her well-being. This wasn't the same as leading a unit, as taking care of my guys. This was a little girl, a child who would rely on me for everything.

Then another thought came unexpectedly. *I missed so much.* She was seven years old and we were strangers, expected to now live together, share a living space and a home. To learn to love each other.

Shit, I'm not ready.

It was a lot to take in, and I gave myself a long moment to think. To plan.

CHAPTER 13
BRENNA

A child.

Grant is a father. No, not just *a* father, he is the father of this precious little girl with big sad brown eyes. And his identical dimple in her cheek. There it was, the deep dark secret that I'd been waiting for, only it wasn't all that deep or dark. Grant had a surprise kid, that's all.

She looked up at me with curious eyes and gave my hand a small squeeze. Her pigtails were crooked and she had chocolate ice cream smeared across her rosebud lips. "What should we fix first, your pigtails or the chocolate on your face?"

Instead of answering, Mariana swiped the chocolate with the sleeve of her denim jacket and realized her misstep. "Oh. Sorry. Auntie Luna said not to do that."

I shrugged. "That means I get to fix your hair." I turned her around and put her on my lap. "Your hair is beautiful. So soft and thick."

"Are you my new mama?"

"No honey, I'm not. But I can be your friend since it looks like you'll be staying here for a while." I knew Grant well enough to know he wouldn't abandon his child now that he knew about her. "There, your hair is all fixed." I pulled a mirror out of my purse and let her inspect my handiwork.

"Thank you, Miss."

"Call me Brenna. If we're gonna be friends, then you have to call me Brenna."

She turned with a small smile. "I'm a kid. We can't be friends."

"Who says?"

My question confused her and Mariana shrugged. "I dunno, but grownups and kids aren't friends."

"Then maybe you and me can be the first? I don't mind if you don't." The little girls' eyes were so damn sad it was enough to break your heart, and if she needed a friend to ease her pain, I could be that for her. "I'm so sorry about your mama, Mariana. You must miss her a lot."

She nodded and tears formed in her eyes. "I do." The tears fell and I wrapped her little body in my arms, absorbing the pain that shook her tiny frame.

"You know you can always talk about her when the missing gets to be too strong, that way it's like she's still here in a way." I rubbed gentle circles in her back and let her cry on my shoulder until she was all cried out. "That's what I do with my grandmama. I remember her all the time and most days I don't feel so sad."

"You do?" She pulled back to look at my eyes, to make sure I wasn't lying to her.

"Heck yeah, I do. She taught me to line dance and to do

hair, so every day when I go into my beauty salon, it's like she's there with me, laughing at the town gossip and complaining about the pink dye one of my clients requested."

Mariana nodded as if she understood, and I hoped she did, because grief was a son of a bitch that would take you down if given half the chance. "Mama was a bad dancer."

I laughed at her words and noticed the angry, sad woman had returned. "No one is a bad dancer, some just dance to their own beat."

"No, Alyssa was a terrible dancer," the woman added with a sad smile. "But she loved to do it and that made it endearing." She turned her gaze to Mariana. "I've got to get on the road kiddo, but I'm gonna miss you."

"Me too," she said and slid from my lap to wrap her arms around the woman. "Stay here, Auntie Luna. Please."

"I can't. Maybe when I'm done with school I'll find a job close to you and I can bug you all the time."

"Yes, please." The words were muffled against Luna's chest and I could feel the closeness between them, how hard this goodbye was for both of them. "I love you, Luna."

"Love you too, honey bunny. Forever and always." Luna smacked a kiss on each cheek and took a step back, almost as if she knew that if she didn't go now, she might never leave. She shooed her towards me with a sad smile. "Be good for your father."

"Okay."

Luna looked at me. "She likes you and she doesn't normally do well with new people. Be kind to her, none of this is her fault."

"We're already friends," I assured the woman. "Just like

me and Grant. I'll keep an eye on her, but she's his, not ours."

Luna nodded. "If you say so. Talk to you soon, kiddo." She walked across the backyard looking so sad and lonely that I couldn't take my eyes off her. What kind of love did it take to do what was best for another person, no matter how much it hurt you? I had a feeling that despite her angry exterior, Luna was one hell of a woman.

Mariana squeezed my hand again and I looked down at her. "You know what helps when I'm feeling sad? Chocolate."

She grinned. "That's what Mama and Auntie Luna say too."

"Well, we can't all be wrong, can we? Let's go check out that chocolate fountain." We loaded up two plates with dippers and filled our cups with chocolate before finding an empty place to sit. "Cheese? Is that cheese and chocolate?"

For the first time, she laughed, and it was as sweet as my sister's kids. "Yep. It's good, wanna try?" She held out a cube of cheddar. It looked pretty disgusting to me, but I took it and tentatively tasted it. "Good, huh?"

Actually, it was. "Pretty good, Mariana. Weird, but surprisingly tasty. Thanks."

"Welcome," she mumbled and dunked a strawberry into the chocolate, eating with satisfaction. Eventually Grant made his way outside with a hangdog expression on his pale face. The poor guy looked like he'd been run through a washing machine on the cold cycle, stunned and a little shell-shocked. "Uh, hey."

Mariana froze at the sound of his voice and looked up at him. "Hi."

He held out a big hand, his posture hesitant and unsure. "I'm Grant, your dad. You can call me...hell, I don't know. What do you want to call me?"

She shrugged. "Auntie Luna calls you Mr. Lucky."

I snickered and he glared at me. "Definitely not that. We'll figure it out, I guess."

Right. That was my cue to remove myself from this situation before things got out of hand, or more out of hand than they already were. "I should get going." I stood abruptly, but seeing Grant and Mariana together gave me a glimpse of a future I could have, but wouldn't. Not with this man and his daughter, anyway.

"No!" Mariana stood and came to my side. "We didn't finish our chocolate yet."

Dang it, she was right. "But your dad is here now and he's got a much bigger capacity for chocolate than I do, and you don't want to miss out on that." She didn't look soothed, not even a little bit. I dropped down so we were eye to eye and sighed. "You and your father need some time together, to get to know each other. Alone. You know?"

Mariana shook her head, pigtails flying wildly around her head. "I don't think he likes me."

"That's exactly why y'all need to get to know each other. Learn his favorite pizza topping and share your love of cheese and chocolate. You're gonna live together so you have to know each other, Mari. Okay?" She nodded and I wrapped my arms around her. "You know my name, and it's in your dad's phone if you ever need to talk. Okay?"

"Okay. Bye, Brenna."

"I'll see you later, Mariana." I stood and took a step back until my gaze collided with Grant's. He was still stunned, and now he had the wild-eyed look of a cornered animal. "Good luck, Grant."

"You're leaving?"

I nodded. "This has been a shock, and Mariana needs you now." And I needed to save myself from this complicated situation.

"But, what about…us?"

And that look right there, the slightly confused and scared expression told me that escape was my best option at the moment. Grant hadn't given any indication that he wanted more than whatever the hell we were doing together, and the first time he mentions an *us,* is when he's had his life flipped upside down.

"We're still friends, Grant. I just think that you need to adjust to the changes in your life. I'll see you around."

He wanted to say more, I could tell by the determined set of his jaw, and I urged my feet to start moving, to put more distance between us before he convinced me to settle into a life that he didn't really want. Not with me anyway.

So yeah, I made my escape and I did it quickly, marching across the backyard in the same path that Luna had taken a few minutes earlier. Only instead of being sad like Luna, I was disappointed as hell. Things were going well with Grant, at least I'd convinced myself they were, but the appearance of Mariana brought home the truth.

We were just screwing around. There was nothing serious between us, no potential for a future relationship and I'd been fooling myself about that. About what I really wanted from Grant and most of all, about what he was willing and able to give.

That little girl had just saved me a world of heartache, and I vowed to keep my promise to her. I couldn't be anything but her friend, but I would be that for her, for as long as she needed me.

CHAPTER 14
GRANT

I stood in front of the coffee pot, waiting for it to brew my third cup of the day. It was barely past noon and still, I couldn't manage to keep my eyes open, to focus on anything other than the fact that I hadn't seen Brenna since the party. Since the day I found out that I had a seven year old daughter.

I missed her. Unbelievably, I missed her. I'd made sure that I never let a woman ever become so important to me that I missed her when she was gone, and here I was on a Monday afternoon, missing Brenna. Her smile and her laugh, those weird southern sayings she liked to drop like bombs. And most especially that twang that had become so familiar to me.

Did that mean that kids were a dealbreaker for her? I didn't actually know, because she hadn't said, and for the past few days, she hadn't said a damn thing. It had been complete and total radio silence from her.

Nothing. Nada.

"I'm hungry." Mariana's soft voice sounded behind me and pulled me from thoughts of Brenna. I looked behind me to find familiar brown eyes staring up at me. She spoke so infrequently that I wasn't used to the sound of her voice, mostly because she only spoke when she needed something she couldn't get for herself. Otherwise, she stayed in her room. Alone.

Shutting me out.

I turned completely to face her. "What do you want to eat?"

She shrugged. "I dunno. Breakfast."

That wasn't exactly helpful, but I suppose you couldn't say something like that to a little kid. "I usually eat toast with a cup of coffee, Mariana, so what do you normally eat for breakfast?" I didn't think Bread Box was the ideal breakfast for a growing child, and that was what I had when toast and coffee just wouldn't cut it.

Her pink lips parted into a mischievous smile. "Eggs and waffles and bacon!"

"I think there are eggs in the fridge?" My culinary skills would allow me to scramble them or make 'em sunny side up, but that was it. "How does that sound?"

Mariana shrugged, but I didn't miss the disappointed droop to her shoulders. "Fine."

She was too young to know the power that word had when wielded by a woman, but I felt her disappointment viscerally. "All right, let's get some breakfast in your belly."

She flashed a small smile that did nothing to minimize her dissatisfaction before she turned and climbed into a chair at the kitchen table and stared off into space. Utterly silent.

The doorbell sounded and as much as it shamed me, I took the out it gave me with a sigh. On the other side of the door was Miles and Shannon, wearing matching, worried smiles. "Hey guys. What are you doing here?"

Shannon took a hesitant step forward and scanned the hall with a smile. We just came to check on you guys, to see how you were settling in?"

"Are you asking me if that's why you came?"

"No," she sighed and shook her head. "I insisted we come to check on you guys. So, how's it going?"

I took a step back and waved Miles inside. "Honestly? Not good. I'm pretty sure she hates me and doesn't trust me as far as she can throw me." It was like pulling teeth to get her to even acknowledge me, and when she did, it was as if Mariana was scared of me for some reason. I was half tempted to call Luna and demand she admit all the horrible shit she must have said about me.

Shannon nodded around a sigh, rubbing her belly and lost in thought. "She needs time, Grant. I know you're used to your charm working on every female from age zero to ninety-nine, but this isn't the same. She's lost her mother and her godmother, it's a lot of change for kid. She needs you to be kind and patient and loving. Most of all, she just needs you to be there. Always there."

"I am." That was about the only thing I was good at, showing up and being there. The rest would take some time. And plenty of effort.

"Good." She gave my chest a pat and gifted me with a wide, warm smile. "I brought brunch."

"You are the best, Shannon!" I pulled her into a hug,

ignoring the disapproving groan from Miles. "What did you bring?"

"Let's find Mariana and see."

Giggles sounded from the kitchen, a sound that surprised me, but not as much as finding the little girl wearing a bright smile as she chatted on the phone. On. The. Phone. "You gonna come over?"

Shannon smiled and turned to me. "She's already making friends? That's good."

I shrugged. "If so, it's news to me. We haven't been anywhere other than your party and a big box store since she got here. Maybe it's Luna."

"Interesting." Miles stroked his chin, smiling as if Mariana's smile was contagious.

"Okay," she said and bopped her head from side to side. "I won't forget. Mmm-hmm, I promise." She nodded even though the person on the other end of the call couldn't see her. "Bye Brenna. See you soon, right?"

Brenna? The same Brenna who basically ghosted me since the party this past weekend? I figured she vanished because of Mariana, but here she was, chatting like they were old friends. Which meant it was me. Right? I looked back at Shannon who wore an equally shocked expression. Miles held up his hands in a *don't ask me* gesture.

"You guys are a big damn help."

"I'm still hungry," Mariana said unceremoniously, a hint of a pout in her tone.

Shannon laughed. "I guess it's a good thing I brought mini breakfast burritos, isn't it?"

Mariana gasped. "You did?"

"Yep. Do you like breakfast burritos?"

Mariana nodded. "Does it have cheese 'cause I love cheese." She arched her brows and waited for Shannon to put the Bread Box bag on the table. "All kinds of cheese," she clarified.

Shannon laughed. "I think we're gonna be good friends, kiddo. I love cheese too. All kinds." She put two miniature burritos on the plate in front of Mariana before the rest of us sat down and ate in a satisfied silence, which gave me plenty of time to think.

Why was Brenna ignoring me?

What had I done to piss her off?

I had no answers, not yet, but I made a planned to get some answers.

CHAPTER 15
BRENNA

The salon was busier than ever today with half the chairs occupied, mostly with walk in clients and I should have been thrilled. I *was* thrilled to bits, but I didn't feel like myself. My spark was missing and I knew why. In one word, Grant.

I missed him. I missed the sound of his laughter, his handsome face, the way his eyes twinkled with mischief, and even the way he teased me about my accent, which I knew he secretly loved. I just plain missed him, and that fact, well is made me mad. Spittin' mad if you want to know the truth. I had to keep my distance, no matter how bad the longing got, no matter how many ways I convinced myself that one little phone call wouldn't hurt.

I knew it would, and I was determined to keep my distance, so I focused instead on the gossip being bandied about the salon.

"Ten bucks and my blueberry pie says Stone and Sophie will have a beautiful little girl." Shirl's voice was more wistful than anything, and I wondered if she had any grandchildren of her own.

"I'll take that bet. I've already got twenty on Mara being pregnant before year's end, and I have a feeling I'm gonna cash in big!" I zoned out again so I couldn't say who took Shirl's bet, but I let the gossip bounce off me as I set curls, washed hair and clipped split ends until I was blue in the face.

It was a good day at work, no, it was a great day at work, but I just wasn't in the head space to enjoy it, and that just directed all my anger at a certain former SEAL who occupied my thoughts nonstop. By the time the first and second wave of customers cleared out, it was past lunch time and I was cranky and starving, what some of the girls called 'hangry'. But the two remaining clients were nurses who worked the overnight shift and were desperately in need of some pampering, so I did my best to give them what they needed while I counted down the minutes until I could grab some food.

They were both almost finished and the end was in sight, I could practically taste the hot, greasy lunch I planned to enjoy at the diner, and then the bell sounded over the door. Another client. After a frustrated sigh, I pasted on a smile and shouted a welcome to the newcomer.

"Be with you in a sec!"

"You get to make people look pretty all day?" Mariana's voice was unexpected, and I turned to find her big brown eyes trained on me in wonder. She looked so small with her oversized purple backpack, which she tossed on a chair with a very grownup sigh. "Cool."

"Mariana, what are you doing here?" I glanced at the clock with a frown. "Shouldn't you be in school right now?"

She nodded, her expression going from wide-eyed wonder to annoyance. "I don't like that school, or the kids. Or the teachers. They're weird and they stare too much, and I'm not going back."

I couldn't help but laugh at her stubborn insistence. "I'm sorry to tell you, but kids your age have to go to school or else your parents get in trouble with the law."

"I'm just one kid," she groaned and flung herself into a chair with the drama of a teenager.

"Maybe so, but the government won't see it that way. How about you give the school and the kids a chance? Let them get to see what a cool little girl you are."

Mariana shook her head vehemently. "Why do I need them as friends when I have you?"

"Because you'll be spending a lot of time in that building, and friends are useful to have in school. Makes the day go by faster."

"I can work here." She looked around the salon with confidence. "You need help?"

I shook my head and gave the nurses one final spritz before sending them on their way. Then, I turned my attention back to Mariana. "I always need help, but there are laws about employing underage people and you, my friend, are far too young to hold a job."

"But I used to help Mama sweep up all the time. And wash counters." I could hear the whine creep into her voice, and I had to bite back a laugh at the feisty little girl. "I can do lots of grown up chores."

"And I'll be happy to let you, but after the school day is over."

"Ugh, fine." She grunted and rolled her eyes. "What do you do now that the customers are gone?"

"Usually I would clean, but I'm tired and hungry, so grab your bag because we're going to the diner."

"We are? Can I get a cheeseburger with bacon? And chili?" Her eyes lit up with excitement the way only men and little kids did at the mention of food and she began to hop up and down, the first signs she showed of being an actual child rather than a sad girl with the weight of the world on her shoulders.

"Where would you put that much food?"

She giggled and pat her belly. "My tummy, of course. So, can I?"

"If you eat a salad or bowl of soup first, sure." We got to the diner and found a booth overlooking the main street. "You know you can't keep leaving school, don't you? At some point they'll call your daddy and he'll be upset about it."

She shrugged and let out a long-suffering sigh. "He won't care. He doesn't even want me around."

"I'm sure that's not true, Mari. Your father is just used to being good at everything, and he's probably not sure he knows how to be good at being a dad." At least I hoped that was it, and not that he really didn't want to be a father to his own child.

"Nobody's good at everything." She said the words as if she had heard them a million times, probably from the lips of her mother.

I laughed at her wise words. "If you listen to my sister,

she'll tell you that nothing teaches you that lesson like parenthood."

"You have a sister?"

"Yep, she's three years younger than me. Married with two kids and another on the way." I still couldn't believe Jessie May was having another kid, it was like the lovebirds couldn't keep their hands, or other body parts, to themselves.

"I always wanted a kid sister, but I would even take a little brother. Mama said I was all the kid she needed, but it would've been nice." The sadness had returned, and my heart ached for her, which was the only explanation for why I let her order that giant burger she would never be able to finish.

We were half way through our food when Shannon called. "Hey Shannon, what's up?"

"I need your help, well not me, Grant actually." There was panic and worry in her voice and I sat up taller.

"Why? What's going on?"

"It's Mariana, she must have snuck out of school and now no one knows where she is."

My shoulders relaxed and I shook my head at her from across the table, mouthing the worlds, "You're in big trouble," to her. "It's all right Shannon, I know where she is. Found me on my way to the diner and she's inhaling a burger right now."

"Oh, thank god! Grant is going crazy!"

But he didn't bother to ask for my help, which made me sad. "I'll drop her off as soon as we finish eating. Will you let him know?" There was no way to get out of seeing him all too soon, but I was happy to put it off for as long as I could.

"Yeah, sure," she sighed. "Is everything good with you guys?"

"Yep. Just peachy."

"That's a lie, but there are three big bad SEALs going crazy over a missing little girl. Talk soon." The call ended and I stared at Mariana until she cracked.

"You've been reported missing, little girl. Prepare yourself for a lot of trouble."

"Yeah, so what? I don't know anyone here but you and *him*, so it's the same as being in trouble anywhere."

I couldn't really argue with that logic. "You say that now, wait until you're sent to bed with no dessert, you can't watch any TV, and you're forced to watch sports with your daddy."

"Ugh!" She picked up the burger and took another oversized bite that left a ring of chili sauce around her mouth. "So good."

It looked really good. "I'll trade you a bite of that burger for a bite of potato nachos."

"Deal!" Her wide, chili stained smile flashed adorably as she pushed her plate towards me and waited expectantly for me to do the same.

We ate in a satisfied, grunt filled silence until both plates were clean. "Ready to face the firing squad, Mari?"

She shrugged. "Don't matter to me."

"We'll see about that. Come on." We went back to my car and I drove Mariana to the house on the lake, taking my sweet time to delay adding any more sadness to her young life. But, as with all things, you can only delay them, not put them off forever.

So, we both went inside, where Grant waited for us.

"Mariana! Where have you been? I thought someone had kidnapped you, dammit." His big hands gripped her shoulders, his face filled with worry and anger. "What were you thinking?"

She shrugged out of his grip. "I don't like it here, and you don't want me here anyway. Just do what you're gonna do." Her amber brown eyes glanced up at me. "We'll still be friends, won't we?"

"You bet."

Grant let out a groan of frustration, put his hands on his knees and pushed himself up to his full height. "Go to your room until I've decided what to do with you."

"I'll pack my stuff." Mariana waved at me and then stomped off, as loud as her little legs would allow.

Silence filled the room, thick and tense as Grant turned his full attention to me. "Thanks for bringing her home."

"No problem. Happy to help." That wasn't quite as awkward as I thought it would be, which made it the perfect time to make my exit. "Good luck."

"You haven't called." His words stopped me before I made it to the door, and I let out a deep exhale before turning to face him.

"Neither have you. Not even when Mariana went missing."

"I'm not the one who walked away." He shook his head and shoved his hands deep in his pockets. "Why did you walk away, Brenna?"

"To protect myself. Obviously."

"From me?" He seemed genuinely shocked, which was about what I expected from him.

"Certainly not from Mariana." Although I should have

considered that too, letting the little girl worm her way into my heart was bound to leave me with an even bigger heartache.

"I thought maybe you left because of her."

"I did, just not how you're thinkin'." I folded my arms across my chest and sighed. "We were having fun, Grant. Things were casual and it worked for us, for both of us. I knew you didn't want anything serious, and I was having enough fun with you that it didn't matter. Figured I'd let things play out however they would, because it wouldn't last too long."

"You weren't in a hurry for anything serious."

"With you? No. But that doesn't mean I don't want to meet the right man one day and fall in love, have kids, the whole dang shebang. But you're fun and gorgeous and I like you, so I figured, what's the harm."

"Until it turns out I have a kid? Then you bolt like your ass is on fire. Right?" The anger in his voice kicked up a notch and I laughed. At first it was just a bark of laughter and then it was a full bellied laugh.

"No. Until you start throwing around words like 'us' when you'd never mentioned us being an official 'us' until Mariana came into your life. I'm not going to be with you just because you need help adjusting to your new role as a daddy, Grant. And I'm certainly not gonna let myself believe you suddenly want more and you want it with me, because of her." My heart raced at finally getting those words out, finally telling him the truth instead of running from it. From him. "That's why I haven't called."

"Wow. You think I'd use you like that?" He sounded hurt and a blanket of guilt covered me.

I tried like hell to shake it off, though, because he didn't get to be hurt. Not by this. "I don't think you would do it on purpose, but I saw it all play out very clearly Grant."

"Bullshit."

"Okay, since we're being honest, then *you* be honest. How long would this have carried on if Mariana hadn't come into the picture? A month or two? Three, tops?"

"I don't know."

"A few months would mean a few holidays together, maybe a long weekend away. Long enough that this would go from casual to a relationship, and you'd bolt."

"I never promised-,"

"Exactly!" I pointed at him with wide eyes. "Exactly, you never promised anything, and I never asked you to, but I walk away and you want to know *what about us?* What about an *us* that never really was? What else should I think?"

"You could have given me the benefit of the doubt, Brenna."

"You're right, I could have, and I'm sorry that I didn't. But I'm not in the market for another broken heart, Grant. I'll see you around." That wasn't as bad as I thought, but I could've gone my entire life without having this conversation, without having it laid so bare, just how unimportant I was to him.

He didn't even try to deny that our relationship, casual as it was, wouldn't have gone anywhere. It was a fact. Grant was great, a good guy who was always up for a good time. But he was an easy guy to fall for, and the easy ones were always trouble.

Always.

Grant came to the front door just as I slid behind the steering wheel. "This conversation isn't over, Brenna."

I flashed a small, sad smile. "Yeah Grant, it is. Goodbye."

He smiled. "See you soon."

That sounded more like a threat than a promise.

CHAPTER 16
GRANT

"It's not like she was working all that hard to try to be my girlfriend. Most women drop hints like bombs when they're ready for more, but did she? No! She never once asked for a drawer at my place, to meet my parents or any of the other crap women do when they mark their territory. So how am I the bad guy?" Brenna's words haunted me and I could not stop thinking about them, no matter how hard I tried. "Well?"

Liam groaned and slid his pen across the conference room table before he reached for a cronut. "I guess it's safe to say we won't get any work done until we work this out for him."

"I don't need you to work out a damn thing, just help me understand. What did I do wrong?" I shook my head. "And that's the worst part, she was all calm and sympathetic, like she felt bad for me. The least she could have done is make me feel like an asshole."

Miles snickered. "Seems to me she did that just fine.

You're wearing the stink of guilt pretty successfully from where I'm sitting."

"Seriously?" I couldn't believe they were having such fun at my expense when I was clearly distraught.

"Look Grant, let me ask you something." Liam sat a little taller and his gaze met mine.

"All right. Ask."

"Is Brenna wrong?"

That was the question I'd been asking myself all night, that was my focus, instead of how I should punish Mariana for leaving school grounds and scaring the hell out of me. "Yes, she's wrong. I like her and I thought we were having a good time. Just because I asked what about us when I did, doesn't mean Mariana is the only reason I said it." That was ridiculous. I wasn't looking for a wife, and certainly not just for my daughter.

"Maybe," Miles began with a sympathetic shrug. "Maybe not. But the timing can't be coincidental, and I don't think Brenna is wrong for thinking it might be a little *too* coincidental."

"You too, Miles? I can't believe you or Brenna think so little of me. You actually think I would use her just to help me out with Mariana?"

Liam barked out a laugh that seemed to bounce off every wall in the conference room. "You wouldn't be the first man to do it, Grant. And before Mariana came along you were happy to keep things casual, and you liked the fact that Brenna didn't push you for more."

"But that's the point," I growled back. "She never pushed for more and now she's gone because I'll never want more, and if I do, it's only because I need a mother figure for my child supposedly. That's crap logic and you know it."

"Maybe she did want more, but she knew she wouldn't get it from you, so she decided you were good enough for the moment." Miles shrugged. "Women do that, apparently."

I nodded and let out a long, frustrated sigh. "That's pretty much what she said, and I still say it's bullshit."

"Why now, Grant? Why do you suddenly want more than a casual fling with Brenna? If it has nothing to do with Mariana, what does it have to do with?" Liam's gaze was strong and unflappable. "Worried no woman will want to deal with a single father who can't stay out late?" He let out a loud, barking laugh meant to piss me off, which he succeeded at doing.

"Asshole."

"No arguments from me," Liam said with a grin. "Can we get back to work now, or are we gonna paint each other's toenails?"

At Liam's teasing words, we spent the next seventy-five minutes going over actual business issues that needed to be addressed, including another trip for Miles to the east coast for more sign ups. It was productive, and I appreciated the guys trying to help with my Brenna situation, even if they just muddied the waters even more.

Back in my office, I tried to focus on outlining an easier version of our teamwork obstacle course for a few upcoming corporate clients, but all I could think about was Brenna and that damn sad smile she wore as she left the lake house last night. "This is ridiculous." I couldn't just let myself be distracted by a woman all day, not when I had work to do here and a whole different set of chores to take care of when I got home. Mariana was self-sufficient, but she was still a child who needed her meals cooked, her laundry washed and her homework checked over. There was no time for me to be distracted. I picked up the phone.

"Grant, what's up?" Her voice was even, not happy or sad to hear from me, just a hint of surprise.

"What's up is that I can't get you or your words, out of my head, Brenna. What are we going to do about that?"

She let out a pretty, feminine laugh. "We aren't going to do anything, Grant. Neither of us."

I frowned and tried to understand if I'd heard her right. "Why not?"

"Because," she sighed. "We've already been over this, Grant. We've had our fun, but it's time for you to focus on Mariana. It's time for us both to move on."

I was losing her, I could feel it, and worse, I didn't like it. "What if I don't want to move on from you, Brenna. We had a good thing, didn't we?"

"It was perfect, Grant. For what it was, it was absolutely perfect."

"You mean for the temporary relationship that it was?"

"Yeah," she sighed. "That's exactly what I meant. Why are you so determined to make this a big thing? You got exactly what you wanted and yeah, it might have ended sooner than either of us liked, but that's where it was always gonna end up."

"You don't know that," I insisted.

"I absolutely do." She let out a nervous laugh and I could picture her in my mind, running her fingers through long blond locks. "You don't want me, Grant. Not before Mariana and not now. I'm a familiar face and we have good chemistry, but if you wanted me, you would have wanted me before now."

"I do want you, dammit!"

"For sex, and that's all right. I enjoyed that part of our relationship too, but we have to be smart. Eventually we can be friends and we'll need to be, because it takes a village to raise a child and I plan to be part of that village."

"Even if we're not together?"

"Yes, Grant. Even though we are not together. At some point we'll both move on and find ways to behave like adults. To pretend we've never seen each other naked."

"Impossible."

She laughed. "Well, we can both try. Really hard. That's why the good lord above invented alcohol." Her laughter went on for a few more moments but it wasn't true laughter, it was meant to fill the void, to avoid talking about the thing she wanted to ignore. Us. The heat and the chemistry between us.

Nothing else was working, maybe the truth would. "I wasn't trying to take our relationship to the next level or anything, Brenna. I just meant that we're friends and usually friends chip in to help out in these situations."

This time her laugh was genuine. "I might have believed you if it hadn't taken you a week to come up with that answer, Grant. I'm not upset."

"You're not?"

"No. Maybe a little disappointed that things ended so soon and so abruptly, but I'd rather they end now before I end up falling for you."

"Would it be so bad if you fell for me?"

"Yes, Grant. It would be, because you wouldn't fall for me. You wouldn't love me."

"I could."

"I believe that because you're a kind and sweet and passionate man, Grant Lopez. But the truth is that you wouldn't. You won't." She let out a soft sigh that hit me right in the chest. "I have to go, Grant. Bye."

She ended the call before I could come up with another response, another point that might make her reconsider, because dammit I missed her.

CHAPTER 17
BRENNA

I stood in line at Bread Box, tapping my foot and nibbling on one of my newly painted hot pink nails, impatient as ever while waiting for a group of tourists to finish jaw-jacking to Mara. Why in the hell were there so many tourists in town today, anyway? Pilgrim was a town that loved to have festivals, concerts, carnivals and any other reason to get together with food, booze and baked goods. I loved that about this town, but right now, I resented these non-locals keeping me from my pastries.

"Next!" Mara's loud voice had my sneakered feet advancing to the counter and I ignored the worried dip of her brows. "What'll it be?"

"A box of mix and match, a dozen please. Wait, no, better make it the eighteen pack. Yeah, that's what I want. Eighteen mix and match, please. Thanks."

Mara tilted her head to the side, staring at me like I just parked my spaceship in front of the bakery. "Everything all right, Brenna?"

"Yep, just peachy. Why do you ask?"

Mara let out a bark of laughter. "Maybe because you've been tapping your foot like a fiend since you got in line and now, you're asking for enough pastries to feed you for a week. Wanna talk about it?"

Nope. Absolutely not. "Nothing to talk about, but thanks." When I was down, I indulged in sugar and butter and flour, of all varieties. Cakes and cookies and pies, tarts or cupcakes, I loved them all.

"Right. Give me a second," she said and disappeared into the kitchen before I could tell her I wasn't going anywhere until I got my box of goodies.

A few seconds later, Shannon pushed through the doors with a worried smile. "Hey, let's chat while Mara gets your order together."

"Not necessary, but sure." I turned back to Mara and glared. "Narc."

"Unapologetically so," she said with a shrug and a wink.

I followed Shannon to a table close to the counter just in case another rush of tourists came in and dropped down. "What's up?"

"You're upset about Grant." It wasn't a question and it didn't need to be, because clearly I was upset. "Talk to me, Brenna."

"Nothing to talk about. We talked about it and agreed that we should be friends." That was a loose interpretation of what happened, but in time, Grant will come around to my way of thinking. I was sure of it.

"You both agreed?"

"Basically, yeah." He didn't get it now, but in no time

there would be another woman warming his bed. "It's no big deal, Shannon. Really."

"Eighteen pastries is a big deal, Brenna, at least admit that much."

"Fine, I'm wallowing, but only for today and then I'll be done with it. Over it. Like it never even happened."

She sighed as she sat back and rubbed her growing baby bump. "That's not really a thing, you know that right?"

"What I know is that I'm trying to be an adult about this. It stings, but only a little bit right now, so I'll do the girly thing and eat my weight in sugar, and when the sun rises tomorrow, I'll push my shoulders back and the world will be like it was before." Before Grant.

"Or you could just give Grant a chance to prove he is who you think he is."

I shook my head. "No, I can't do that. I'm done making bad decisions because I hope they'll end up being good decisions in the end. He didn't want me for anything more than some fun before he found out about his daughter, and if I gave this, us a shot, I'd always wonder if I was there because Mariana needs a mother. I can't do that to myself."

"Sometimes Brenna, men are stupid. They don't know what they want. Or how to ask for what they want, what they need."

"Believe me, I know that. But I also have a bad habit of believing what I want to believe when it comes to my type of man, regardless of what his actions say." I shook my head and stood. "I appreciate the advice Shannon, I really do, but I have to do it this way. For my own protection."

She held up her hands and shrugged. "I had to try, for the sake of you and Grant."

"And I'm happy to have a friend who cares so much, but I'm looking out for my heart this time. Not his."

"You say that now, but you'll change your mind." Mara stared me down as she handed me the box of pastries. "You're like me, hardheaded and determined to do everything the hard way."

"Thanks ladies, but really, I have plenty of pastries to plow through before the day is over. Have a good day." I grabbed the box and rushed from the bakery and ran right into the last person I wanted to see today. "Grant. Mariana. Hey."

"Hi Brenna!" Mariana smiled up at me with a wave. "Whatcha got in there?"

"A little of this and a little of that. Where are you going looking so colorful?" She had on a rainbow hoodie, blue jeans and hot pink sneakers, and she was adorable.

"We're going to the Book Festival and my dad said I could get five books as long as I promised to read them all!"

"Wow, five whole books? You're gonna be the smartest girl in the whole dang town!"

"Maybe," she said and took my hand in hers, so easy and trusting, the way only kids can trust. "You wanna come with us? It's alright isn't it, Dad?"

Grant blinked, looking dumbfounded by Mariana's question. "Uh, well I guess that depends on Brenna."

It was the perfect out. "Sorry, I have a bunch of house stuff to catch up on today, but you two have fun." Grant didn't want me there any more than I wanted to be, and besides all that, my pastries were getting cold. "If you see anything on new hairstyling techniques, think of me, will ya?"

Mari pouted and I already felt myself cracking. "But Brenna, I haven't seen you in forever. Forever," she added with emphasis.

"Forever? I seem to recall you skipped school just a few days ago and scared the bejeezus out of your daddy."

"Okay fine, not *forever*, but it feels like a long time because I lost phone privileges for everyone but Auntie Luna. Say yes, please? Yes! Yes? Yes." Her expression changed with every new way she said the word, almost teasing a smile out of me. "Brenna."

"Okay, fine you little stinker. Let me go put my now ice cold pastries in the car and then I'll meet you guys by the entrance." Maybe they'd get so wrapped up in books they wouldn't notice if I never showed up.

"We can wait here, can't we Dad?"

Grant's lips twitched as if he knew what I was doing, and for good measure he folded those sculpted arms across his chest just to make sure I knew he would offer no help. "Sure, we can wait. As long as it takes."

I arched a brow at them both. "Glad to see you two are already rubbing off on one another. Like father, like daughter."

Mari's giggle followed me down the block and when I turned the corner, I slowed down and allowed myself sixty full seconds to get my racing heart under control. There was no way I could spend the day with Grant and Mari, and not want to be part of their newly formed family. It just wasn't possible, which meant I had to be strong, much stronger than I had ever been when it came to a good-looking man.

I sucked in several deep breaths and let each one out slowly, and all the tension and disappointment I felt about how things had turned out with Grant right along with them. Today was about showing Mariana a good time.

That was all.

"All right. I'm ready." I squared my shoulders and stood tall, walking like a royal as I joined the twosome in front of the bakery. "Who's ready to find some cool books?"

"Me!" Mari's excitement and her nonstop chatter made things a lot easier, keeping the focus off me and Grant and the tension that stood between us like a living, breathing person. "What kind of books do grownups read?"

"Romance and mysteries," I told her. "Sometimes I like mysteries with a hint of romance."

"Yuck," she said with certainty. "Mama loved fairytales, said they were proof that sometimes things did work out in the end."

"She sounds like a very smart woman," I told her and gave her shoulder a small squeeze.

"She was really smart." Sadness crept into her voice and I elbowed Grant.

"What?" He mouthed the word silently.

"Say something. Your favorite books," I mouthed back, punctuating the words with an eyeroll.

"I like sports history books, biographies and mystery books. Sometimes I like to read science fiction, but don't tell anyone I said that. Either of you." He pointed at us both, a fake threatening look on his face.

"I won't tell," Mari promised and made an 'x' over her heart.

"I make no such promise," I teased. "It sounds like the perfect piece of intel that could be useful at a later date."

"You wouldn't dare."

I shrugged. "I might. Depends on what kind of favor I need and how insistent you are that you won't do it. Otherwise, your secret is safe-ish with me."

"Good to know." He winked and bumped my shoulder. "Guess I'll just have to figure out a way to make you promise to keep that pretty little mouth shut."

And just like that, I wanted him.

Again.

CHAPTER 18
GRANT

"You're good with her." Brenna wore a small smile as she looked at Mariana skipping ahead of us through the Book Festival, smiling and waving at all the new faces who stopped to greet her.

I shrugged off the compliment, but coming from Brenna, I let the words sooth my self-doubts. "We're a work in progress most days. Sometimes she calls me 'Dad' with this kind of unsure voice that reminds me we're basically strangers. Then sometimes, she calls me Grant like we're old friends. It's strange."

She let out a throaty laugh and let one hand drop to my shoulder, causing an undeniable zing to shoot through me. "That pretty much sums up parenting if you ask my sister. Strange."

"Yeah?" It was nice to hear that my struggles weren't necessarily due to my own shortcomings.

She nodded and ran a hand through her blond hair, today styled in springy curls that gave her a sexy girl next door quality, it was even more appealing than the sexy cowgirl look. "Oh yeah. I swear half the time I only look forward to her calls to hear all the crazy things the kids get up to. Molly Ann went through a phase where she called her Jessie May instead of Mama, and I thought my cool-headed sister would blow a gasket!" She laughed again at the memory and my longing for her shot high up into the sky.

"I missed this," I told her in a moment of honesty. "Just talking to you and listening to your laugh. It's nice."

Her laughter faded, but the smile remained, small and wistful. "It *is* nice."

"We could hang out sometime, you know. As friends."

She flashed a wide, knowing smile at my words. "I think we both know that there's no way in hell we could ever be *just* friends. I like you Grant, probably more than it's wise to like you, given…everything. Let's not ruin it."

"But what if we made it better?" It wasn't unheard of to like the woman you were sleeping with, I always did, but it wasn't the same with Brenna. I genuinely enjoyed her company and looked forward to any time I got with her, naked or clothed.

"How would we do that?" I should have expected the question, this was Brenna we were talking about, but it took me too long to answer and she laughed. "Can't come up with anything other than sex?"

"No, it's not that. I'm just trying to figure out how to explain it. This is all kind of new to me, Brenna."

"I know." Her voice was full of sympathy, as if she felt sorry for me, a grown ass man who couldn't put his feelings into words.

"Hey Brenna?" Mariana tugged on her hand with a shy

smile. "Have you read this book?" She held up a copy of *Charlotte's Web*.

"I have and I love it. It's about an unlikely friendship between a pig and a spider."

Mariana turned her big brown eyes onto me, uncertain as she prepared to make her request. "Can we get this one, Dad?"

As if I could deny her anything when she made a sincere request, and her sweet voice reminded me of how important my new job was to both of us. "Of course. Keep looking to see if you find any others." She ran off and I let out a sigh, unaware I'd been holding my breath.

"You love her." Brenna's words weren't in the form of a question, they were stated as fact.

"I do. It hasn't been long at all, but I love her already." My eyes went wide at the shock in my own voice. "I don't mean that I didn't think I would, just-,"

"You didn't think it would happen so fast?"

I nodded, stunned by the relief that coursed through me at her quick understanding. "Yeah. I thought it would happen over time because I wasn't expecting her, I didn't have nine months to look forward to meeting her and falling in love with the idea of her." Brenna's blond brows arched in my direction. "I've been watching a lot of Netflix."

Her giggle was worth the embarrassment at my moment of raw honesty. "Good for you. It shows how much it means to you to be a good father. I'm happy for both of you."

"Most days I feel like I'm doing it wrong."

"That's normal I hear, and it's how you know you're doing it right." Brenna bumped her shoulder against mine, her smile encouraging. "Keep trying and keep showing up. She's already warming up to you."

"Is she?" I shrugged, not used to feeling to unsettled around any female, let alone one I was now in charge of. "Half the time I think she's waiting for me to tell her she can't have something, and the other half I think she's surprised that I'm still here."

"Loss will do that to a kid. It's not you, Grant. It's losing her mother. It's up to you now to teach her that everyone doesn't leave."

"You're pretty smart, you know that?" And when she fluttered her eyelashes prettily, it brought home that she wasn't just smart, she was also beautiful and funny. And intoxicating.

"I found two more Dad, is that okay?" Mariana looked up at me expectantly, waiting for me to tell her she was costing too much, asking too much, and it broke my heart a little.

"On one condition," I told her with a smile.

"What's a condition?" Her gaze bounced between me and Brenna, confusion dipping her dark brows into a frown.

"It means you can get the books, but only if you agree to my thing."

She took a wary step back and nodded. "Okay."

"We read them together." All the parenting books I'd read said it was important to have routines and to spend time together each day, just the two of us.

"That's it? You want to read these kid books with me?" I nodded and her confusion deepened. "Why?"

"Because my mom used to read with me and we had a good time. She would do voices and dramatic pauses, and when I was a little older than you are now, she would ask me questions about the stories and we would make up our own. I thought maybe we could do something like that."

"Really?"

"Yeah, Mariana, really."

It came slowly, but the smile that spread across her face was genuine. "That sounds like fun."

"Good." I held my hand out for the books and went to make the purchase, glancing over my shoulder occasionally to see her and Brenna deep in conversation about something. "Okay, what's next?"

"I'm hungry," Brenna said abruptly.

"Me too!" Mariana jumped up and down. "They have fried tacos here," she said to Brenna. "Fried. Tacos."

Brenna took Mariana's hand in hers. "Oh honey, you're just learning about birria tacos? Then let me be your teacher, because you're in for a real treat." Mariana looked up at her like she was the wisest woman in the world, eyes full of wonder and anticipation. "I don't know about you, little girl, but I love food that lets me be my messy self."

"You like to be messy?"

"Oh yeah. I despise having to be all prim and proper when I eat, especially when I'm crazy hungry. Like now." She bent down and whispered the last two words like they were conspiring together and Mariana ate it up.

"Me too. I'm *starved*," she said dramatically.

Brenna looked over at me and shrugged. "You heard the girl, Grant. Feed us."

It took about five minutes, but we found the infamous fried taco stand and then a small table where the two females devoured their food, mostly in silence. "Oh. My.

God. This is *soooo* good," Mariana proclaimed after her second taco, her smile stained with the red dipping sauce.

"Right?" Brenna let out a laugh around another bite of taco, and then returned to her role as teacher. "Now, when you get near the end, tip the bowl like this so you can dip the taco and pick up the little bits and bops at the bottom."

Mariana followed suit and groaned. "Yum!" She looked to me and her smile widened. "Do you like it Dad?"

"Not as much as you two, but it's delicious."

Brenna scoffed. "Your father was in the Navy, and he's used to things being neat and tidy. These tacos probably offend his sense of order."

"It does?" Her innocent question brought a smile to my face.

"I'm just used to doing things a certain way, that's all. But I was in the military because I believe that you should enjoy things the way you like, as long as you're not hurting anyone. So, get as messy as you want."

Her shoulders fell in relief. "Thank you for your service. Mama says it's important to thank our military for lettin' us be free."

"You're welcome, honey." I risked a look at Brenna who had a hand to her chest, obviously touched by the tender moment.

"You are just the most precious thing ever! I swear." She shook her head and offered up the last fried churro to my daughter. "A reward for being such a sweetheart."

"Thank you, Brenna." She broke it in half and handed part of it back. "We can share."

"What about your dad?"

Mariana smiled. "The sugar and cinnamon is too messy."

Brenna laughed and I couldn't help but join in. "Looks like that dimple and those brown eyes aren't the only thing she inherited from you. Congratulations daddy, it's a smartass!"

"I'm full." Mariana made the pronouncement with a sigh and patted her belly for good measure.

"That's how you know it's time to quit when it comes to birria tacos. A little goes a long way." Brenna wiped her hands and mouth and smiled. "Now it's time to walk off these calories."

"Wait." Mariana mistook her words for a farewell and sat up taller with wide eyes, filled with panic.

"What's up?"

She looked at me and then back to Brenna. "Dad says it's time I make my room my own since I'm staying, and I need some help. Me and Mama didn't get around to that before, you know..."

"I know. What can I do?"

"Take me to pick stuff out for my new room? Dad says that's girl stuff and he's colorblind."

"That explains all the gray and white t-shirts," she said in an amused tone. "Are you sure you want my help? I'm not exactly the style icon of Pilgrim."

Mariana nodded. "You wear what you want, and Mara says it works for you. I want to figure out what I want and what I like too."

"Well now I have to agree, don't I?" She laughed and helped clean Mariana's face. "Sure, honey. Let's figure out a day real soon and have a just us girls shopping day, all right?"

Mariana punched the air. "All right!"

I kept my expression neutral, but I was thrilled Brenna had agreed, because if nothing else, it meant I'd get to see her again.

CHAPTER 19
BRENNA

"What the hell was I thinking, agreeing to this Shannon? It's a recipe for disaster." I sat in my car parked at the end of Grant's driveway, trying to muster up my courage to finish the trip and knock on the door, and more so, preparing myself to see Grant again. "I needed a cold shower after the Book Festival, and we had a tiny chaperone the entire time!"

Shannon's laugh was loud on the phone and I rolled my eyes. "You were thinking that Mariana has been through a lot, and if she decided you're her favorite grownup, that was a good thing."

"Yeah," I sighed. "She's pretty great. But until this moment, I didn't factor Grant into this day. You don't think he'll want to come, do you?"

"Shopping? No. But maybe later, as a thank you?"

"Very funny," I growled, and Shannon only laughed harder.

"Seriously, just say good morning to him, gawk a little, and then grab Mariana and take off for the day."

"Yeah, I can do that. Thanks."

"Good luck today and call me when you get home. Bye."

I shoved the phone in my cupholder and finished the trip to the lake house, walking slowly up the stairs to steel myself for Grant, probably sexy and disheveled first thing in the morning. He opened the door just as I rang the bell.

"Brenna. Good morning."

"Mornin' Grant. Mariana ready?" Yeah, this was easy. I could handle a few seconds, no problem.

"Almost. She had a last minute wardrobe change. Come in?"

"Naw, it's nice. I think I'll enjoy the lake air before we're stuck inside all day. How, uh, are things?"

He smiled as if he knew what I was doing. "Good. Getting better every day. I think so, anyway." He shrugged and took a step onto the porch, his fresh from the shower scent, invading my senses. "How have you been?"

"Good," I sighed. "The salon is busy and that's good, so I'm good." It was painfully awkward between us and I hated that, but it was better than the sparks from the festival. "So, about the shopping today?"

"Right." He produced a credit card and put it in my hand. "She has a full sized bed and a nightstand, but I think she'll need a desk and maybe a dresser?" He sighed and shook his head. "I don't know, Brenna. Get her what you think she needs and try not to max out the card."

I laughed. "That's not what you should tell a woman after you hand her a credit card, but I can work with those limits." He smiled and I smiled back, feeling the pull of attraction between us. I missed Grant too, but those were dangerous thoughts, so when Mariana rushed onto the porch, I allowed myself to relax. A little.

"I'm ready!"

"Perfect. Let's get going so we can shop until one of us drops."

"Okay! Bye Dad!" Mariana ran to the car and hopped in the front seat, capably fastening her seatbelt before she turned to me. "Ready!"

"Have you thought about what you want your room to look like?"

She shrugged. "A little. My old room was really girly with lots of pink and purple everywhere. Mama did it for me and it was nice, but-,"

"But it wasn't you?"

"Yeah," she said in a sad voice. "Is that bad?"

"Nope. We're not miniature versions of our parents, Mariana. We're allowed to be different." I wasn't her mother, just her friend. "Find a way to be yourself, and still honor what your mama meant to you. What does she like?"

"Mama is a girly girl. She likes dresses and lace and makeup and all that stuff. But she also likes crowns and I *love* crowns too!"

"Perfect! I can work with that." We made several stops for bedroom furniture before we got down to the fun part of shopping, the personal stuff. "Okay, we have pillows in all colors, and all of 'em have tiaras on them. What colors do you want?"

Looking more grown up than a seven year old should, Mariana tapped her chin as she examined her options with the seriousness of someone buying a car. She took her time, choosing a black pillow and a royal blue one. "How's that?"

"Do you like it?" She nodded. "Then it's perfect. I'll bet we can find bedding to match."

"Really?" I nodded, and with the giddiness a child her age ought to have, Mariana bounced on her toes. "Cool! Mama always said when money was better she would get me a proper bedroom, but I didn't mind."

"That's because parents always want the best for their kids. My mama couldn't afford much, but she made us pillowcases and curtains, because the fabric was cheaper, and she was an expert with a sewing machine."

"Were you poor too?" Her eyes went wide and Mariana smacked a hand over her mouth. "Sorry."

"Don't be. We weren't just poor, Mariana. My mama would often say we were so po' we couldn't afford the extra 'or', that's how poor we were." I shrugged it off, along with the memories of being the poor kid at school. "It wasn't great, but my mama did her best and it was us girls against the world."

She smiled again. "Us too. Me and Mama and Auntie Luna, us against the world."

"That must be why we like each other so much, we're tough girls."

"Tough girls with tiaras," she said and grabbed the blue bedding dotted with tiaras. "I miss my mama a lot, Brenna."

"Of course you do, honey. You'll miss her every day for the rest of your life, but some day you'll just remember her smile, her off-key singing and the way she made the best burnt toast."

"I won't forget her?"

"Heck no. You'll miss her when you fall in love for the first time, when you have a kid of your own, when you achieve your dreams. She'll be in your heart and your mind on all those occasions, big and small. That's how you keep her alive."

She thought about those words for a long time, staying quiet as I paid and loaded up my car with items for her new life, a life without her mother's physical presence.

"My dad's pancakes are better than mama's, and I love them. Is that wrong?"

"Not at all. Your mama got to bond with you in her tummy, and she got all those years watching you become this great kid, it's only fair that he gets to be the better pancake maker."

"Okay."

"Okay then," I told her as we pulled into the mall parking lot. "What about your walls. Do you want art? Posters of bands and cute boys? Something else?"

She shrugged. "Maybe something with dinosaurs and unicorns?"

"Let's see what we can find and then I need food, or I won't make it much longer. I need fuel."

The sound of her laughter filled me with affection. Was there anything greater than the sound of a child's laughter? "You're only hungry because the food court is right behind you."

I turned and saw she was right. "Maybe."

"Maybe?" The little girl could barely hold back her laughter.

"Do you want to argue, or do you want to get these decoration so we can eat?"

"Dinosaurs and unicorns, then food!"

"Perfect. Come on." After lunch we did a bit more shopping, because what is a day of shopping without a pretty little dress or the perfect pearl snap shirt? For Mariana it was a couple of dresses and the cutest little pair of cowgirl boots. It was the perfect end to the perfect girls' day.

Or maybe, just maybe, I was delaying the inevitable.

Another run-in with Grant.

CHAPTER 20
GRANT

"Why are you in such a hurry to get home?" Liam's voice held a teasing tone, and the mischievous smile he wore told me he was about to give me shit. "Hot date or something?"

I sighed and picked up the bag that held my normal work clothes since I was dressed in STA sweats. "Not a hot date, just a kid who needs to eat and bathe and do homework and all that stuff." That was most of the truth, anyway. The rest of it, that I was rushing home to see if I could spend some time with Brenna before she rushed off, was just for me.

"Do you buy that Miles? Because I don't. In fact, I'm calling bullshit." Liam folded his arms, brows arched in a challenge he knew I couldn't deny. Wouldn't deny.

Miles shook his head. "Yeah, I'm not buying it either. Matter of fact, who's with Mariana today?" His smile was downright devious, and I should have known that Shannon would know, which meant Miles would too.

I shrugged it off like it was no big deal and headed towards the door. "Brenna took her shopping for things to make her feel more at home. Her bedroom still looks like the guest room."

"And that's not something she should be doing with her dad?" Liam stroked his chin comically. "Interesting."

"She likes Brenna, and I figured a woman's input was more necessary than my desire to make her feel welcome in our home." They didn't need to know that it was all Mariana's idea. "Anyway, I have to get going. I need to pick up a few things at the store before I head home, and I don't want Brenna to think I've left her to babysit all day and night."

Liam's voice was loud and booming, echoing through the cavernous hall of the STA building since he followed me towards the door. "And there she is again, Brenna."

"Yeah, that's her name." I glanced down at my watch and back up at my friends. "See you guys tomorrow."

"Good luck," Miles called after me.

"Tell Brenna we said hello," Liam mocked, laughter in his voice.

I flipped them both off and walked a little faster until I was out in the warm, clear day, the last hints of sunshine warming my skin. I made a quick stop at the market for groceries and hurried home, where I was met with the sound of feminine laughter and country music while I unloaded the bags.

"Hey girls, I'm home!"

I was met with silence and then another round of giggles, so I decided to give them a few minutes while I got dinner started, seasoning strips of steak, onions and bell peppers. Then I made my way upstairs, heart thumping in my chest at the thought of seeing Brenna again, and seeing Mariana's new bedroom. I knocked and they both turned at the same time with wide-eyed expressions.

"Hi Dad! Did you see my room? Do you like it?" It was good to see her so excited about staying here with me, for a change.

I scanned the room, noting the shades of blue, with some black and silver that stood in contrast to the pink and purple monstrosity I'd been expecting. They'd done a good job of making the space hers, with throw pillows, tiara accents and a few stuffed animals for good measure. "It's nice," I told her honestly. "Very royal. Are those...dinosaurs?"

Mariana nodded enthusiastically. "And unicorns, because they're my favorite animals."

"Really? Dinosaurs and unicorns?" She nodded again. "Guess that means you won't be bugging me for a pet anytime soon."

Brenna let out a sharp laugh, her blue eyes glittering with amusement.

"Lizards and Komodo dragons are basically dinosaurs, and horses and unicorns are like brothers," she offered with a teasing grin.

Thank goodness for Brenna because I had no comeback for that. "The desk and the chest of drawers will be here in two days."

"Great. Thanks, Brenna. I really appreciate this. Did you ladies have fun today?"

"Oh my god, Dad, we had so much fun!" Mariana bounced up and down like she did a few nights ago when I let her eat chocolate ice cream at nine o'clock at night. "We went to like, five different stores, we had truffles and they were *so* good, and we talked about Mama. That's all right, isn't it?"

"It's more than all right. You can tell me about her anytime you want. You know, she had on a tiara the night I met her. I asked if she was a princess and she laughed, said she was a Queen."

Mariana giggled. "Mama said Queens hold the real power."

Brenna laughed. "Your mama was one smart cookie."

"Yep," she said proudly, staring at Brenna as if she was some kind of superhero.

"We're having steak fajitas for dinner. Who's hungry?"

"Me! I haven't eaten in hours," Mariana declared dramatically.

Brenna tossed her head back and laughed. "We had that street corn right before we left the mall. You've got a hollow leg girl, I swear." She shook her head, blue eyes shining with affection for my kid. "I'll let you two get ready for dinner. I should probably head home."

"You're not staying?" Mariana looked outraged and a little hurt. "You have to say, Brenna. You *have* to. Dad makes the best steak fajitas with his special sauce. You'll love it, I promise."

Brenna clearly wasn't sold, but anything I said would be met with skepticism, and it seemed as if even Mariana knew it, because she blinked those thick, inky eyelashes at Brenna and the woman practically melted. "If they're not as good as promised, you owe me real steak fajitas." I wasn't sure which of us she was talking to, but when she marched out of the bedroom, I was on her heels.

"Are you insulting my fajita-making skills, woman?"

"Not insultin', more like questionin' if you even have those skills." Her sassy response put a smile on my face as I caught up with her.

"I have plenty of skills, Brenna. As you well know." I didn't miss the way her body vibrated, no matter how hard she tried to hide it.

"Yeah, maybe so, but those skills don't exactly translate to cooking delicious fajitas, do they?"

"You guys are being weird," Mariana said, her tone confused and a little grumpy. "Grown ups are really weird. I'm going back to my room."

"Take your new bedding to the laundry room so we can wash it before you use it."

She turned around with a pout. "But I want to sleep on them tonight!"

"And if they get going in the wash, you might be able to." At my words, she took off as fast as her little legs would carry her.

"Good job diffusing that situation."

I sighed. "Like diffusing a bomb."

"Welcome to life with a soon-to-be teenage girl." Her blue eyes bounced around the kitchen. "Need any help?"

"Eye candy is always appreciated when I cook. Have a seat and tell me about your day." It was nice, listening to Brenna's soothing twang while I made dinner, and her loud laughter when she said something that she found funny. "It was sweet of you to tell her that story about her mama. She misses her like crazy."

"I don't know how to do that part. I liked Alyssa, for as little as I knew her, but that's not exactly something you can say to a little kid. Is it?"

"How should I know? I mean, I guess not, but just let her talk, I guess. That's what I did."

Dinner was unlike any dinner my kitchen had seen since it became my kitchen. Mariana talked pretty much non-stop about everything from her new room, the latest dinosaur facts she picked up online, her mother's love of chicken fajitas, and even the "cutest boy ever" on some teen show she liked to watch. It was a nice buffer between me and Brenna, which she clearly wanted, focusing more on the kid than the me.

I didn't let it bother me, at least not now that I understood where she was coming from. I wasn't offended that she thought I wanted her around because of Mariana, because I could admit that *was* a part of it. A small part, but they were already so close that it only made her more appealing.

Mostly, I wanted Brenna for myself though.

And when Mariana fell asleep during a romantic comedy she'd insisted we watch together, I knew my moment to tell her had come. "I'll go put her to bed. Wait for me?"

Brenna stood with a sigh, uncertainty swimming in her eyes. "I don't know, Grant."

"Please."

"Fine." She rolled her eyes and shooed me off and I took off as fast as I could. I traded Mariana's daytime clothes for a pair of red and yellow pajamas that she'd brought with her and wore just about every night.

I wasn't all that surprised to find Brenna putting on her boots when I returned to the living room. "Going somewhere?"

"Yeah. Home. Soon."

"Not too soon, I hope?" I took a step closer and her eyes went wide as she stood and took a step back. "Running, Brenna?"

"I might be. Do I need to run, Grant?" That's what her lush lips said, but the pulse beating a tattoo at her throat said she was just as turned on as I was.

I pressed my body against hers, the hard points of her nipples telling me that my proximity wasn't exactly unwanted. "I really wish you wouldn't run, Brenna. Then again, maybe I'd like to catch you." She sucked in a breath and I couldn't wait another minute, my lips crashed down on hers in a hard, forceful kiss that stole my breath.

Brenna's hands were on the move, one sliding up and down my back while the other gripped a proper handful of my hair as she gave back as intense a kiss as she received. Her tongue danced with mine, and she nibbled my bottom lip until I held her face and devoured her mouth, purring when our tongues touched once again.

A deep, throaty moan rent the air and I pressed my hips against hers, letting her see exactly the effect she was having on me.

"Grant," she said on a breathless whisper, her hands now both gripping my hair, tugging it hard.

"Right here, sweetheart."

"Yeah," she panted. "I can feel you. All of you."

"I'd love to feel all of you, Brenna. Right now." One hand slid up her silky legs. "And this skirt has been on my mind since this morning."

"This ole thing?" She laughed and I swallowed it down, kissing her again because I could do nothing else when she smiled at me like she thought I was more than a good lay, like she thought I was special. "Grant," she gasped when my knuckles scraped against her damp panties.

I didn't wait another minute when her head fell against the wall with a *thud*, I slid her panties to the side and rubbed two fingers against her swollen, wet folds while she moaned sweet little nothings in my ear. She was hot and wet, and it was just for me. A fact confirmed when two honey covered fingers slid deep and she pulsed around me.

"Oh fuck, Brenna."

She laughed and grabbed my wrist. I froze, waiting to see if she would tell me to go to hell, but she didn't. Brenna held my wrist and squirmed and gyrated on my hand, using me for her own pleasure and it was so fucking hot I thought my cock would burst out of my sweats. "Sweet Jesus, you are one dangerous man."

I laughed. "Little ole me?"

She laughed in response and her hands fell away, giving me control of her pleasure again, which I appreciated but it wasn't enough. "Grant, don't tease."

"Never," I growled and nipped her ear. "I want to feel you, Brenna. All of you. The deepest parts of you."

She let out a strangled moan combined with a shaky laugh. "Do you, now?"

"So bad I can taste it." Just to punctuate my words, I slipped my fingers from her body and into my mouth with a moan.

"We can't," she said, her voice filled with disappointment which made me feel a little better. "Not with Mari upstairs."

That was an easy fix. "We can, if you think you can be quiet," I told her with a smile as I led her to the front door, turning left into the guest bathroom instead of the front door.

"Thinkin' awful highly of yourself, aren't you?"

"Hell no, but the sounds you make when you cum, they appear in my dreams damn near every night. I couldn't forget them if I tried, and I don't want to. I want to hear them again. And again." With a soft click, we were locked together in the smallest bathroom in the house.

"Oh, I'll be quiet," she grunted as I peeled red panties off her body, stopping to take a long lick of her honeyed center. "Mostly quiet," she amended with a laugh. A moment later her hands were at my waist, shoving my sweats and boxers down to the floor before taking me in her mouth, hot and deep.

"Oh fuck, Bren!"

She laughed. "I guess we'll both be as quiet as we can."

"Deal." I lifted her against the door and she wrapped long legs around my waist, moaning softly as I lowered her onto my cock.

"Oh, god! Fuck me."

That was the sound I was in search of, the throaty twang that uttered dirty things as she sought her pleasure.

"Harder," she demanded and licked a trail of heat across my lips. "Hard and fast, Grant. Please."

I gave her exactly what she wanted, hell, what we both wanted. We came together hard and fast and deep, and yeah, mostly quiet. Too soon, she pulsed around me, signs of her imminent orgasm. Mine too. "Brenna."

"I feel you," she said with a breathy smile. "Hard and thick. Ready to explode."

I gripped her harder, plunging deep and hard, until she

let out a long, low moan that brought forward my own orgasm. "Brenna!" I kissed her lips because I could, because I wanted to, hell I did it because I was pretty damn powerless to do anything else. The taste of her lips was sweet on my tongue, intoxicating to my bloodstream. I wanted her again. I was still buried inside her convulsing body, and yet I wanted her again.

And again.

Eventually, she pulled back with a satisfied grin that dimmed into something more like a sad smile. She kissed me softly and then gave me a shove before exiting the bathroom. "Good night, Grant."

"Sweet dreams, Brenna." The night didn't turn out exactly how I hoped it would, but it was progress.

Besides, there was always tomorrow.

CHAPTER 21
BRENNA

I paced back and forth inside the empty salon, mind still unable to put together the pieces of exactly how I'd ended up with my skirt hiked up around my waist and Grant surging into my body, when my plan was to get the hell out of there as quickly as humanly possible. But it had happened and it was magnificent.

And a mistake.

A big, fat, horrible mistake.

Because *not* having Grant wasn't ideal, but it was the smart play, to keep my time with him as nothing more than a memory. Having him again only reminded me of what I was missing, and that was just in the bedroom. He'd done his best to flirt with me, to remind me of how much fun we had together when we were fully clothed. All the laughing and smiling and flirting had primed me, I realized for a good night kiss that turned into something else. Something more.

"Okay, I'm here. What's the emergency?" Shannon

waddled into the salon with a concerned, slightly nervous smile. "You look like hell, Brenna. What's going on?"

"I've done something stupid. Something so ridiculously stupid that I can't even piece together how it all happened." I was being dramatic and I couldn't deny that, but it's what the moment called for.

"Well, don't keep me in suspense!"

"I had sex with Grant." It sounded even worse when I said it aloud, like I failed some test.

Shannon's brows pulled together into a confused expression. "And it was horrible? Nowhere near as good as you remember?"

I huffed out a laugh. "God, I wish! That would make all of this bearable, at least."

She sighed and ran a hand through thick red hair. "So you called me over here because you had hot sex with a hot guy that you really like?"

I folded my arms, offended. "It sounds silly when you put it like that."

Shannon blinked innocently. "Is that not what happened?"

"Yes, and no! You know damn well why this is a problem, Shannon. I'm sorry if you were busy or if you're unwell from the pregnancy, I wasn't thinkin' clearly. If you have someplace else to be, I won't be offended." Jessie May always said when I was in a tizzy I couldn't see beyond my own personal problems.

"No, I'm sorry," she sighed, looking truly apologetic. "It's fine. That's what friends are for, right?"

"Only if that's what they want to be."

Guilt flashed across her face and, dammit, that just

made me feel worse. "I do. I swear." We stared at each other for a long time, tension and uncertainty brewing between us and I hated that.

I sighed and shook my head. "No, it's fine. You're right, it's no big deal. Good sex is never a problem. Right?" I flashed a bright smile, hoping to sell the story that I was fine handling my own problems.

"Come on, Brenna. Talk to me. I know you think you should keep your distance from Grant, but obviously that isn't happening. Why are you fighting it so hard?"

"Because I have to. Grant is great, he would be everything I wanted in a man except he doesn't want a long-term commitment. He only wants me now because I get along with his daughter and he hasn't quite found his footing as a father yet." When he did, his interest would wane, and I'd be left with nothing but wasted time and a broken heart.

"Other than the day he was smacked upside the head with the news that he was a father, has Grant given you any other indication that he only wants you to be a mom to his kid?"

"Well, no. But before she came along he was mister cool and breezy, no need to put labels on things because we're just having fun."

"And now?" One perfectly sculpted brow arched in question.

"And now he's saying things like he misses me, thinks about me and can't resist me. It's unsettlin'."

"It could be unsettling and true, couldn't it?" Shannon's gaze stared a hole right through me and I let out an annoyed sigh.

"It could be, but I'm too scared to let it all be wrapped up into a messy tangle that will be impossible to get myself out of when it all goes to hell."

"*If* it all goes to hell, because there's no guarantee that it will." She pursed her pink lips into a triumphant smile, both hands resting on her rounded belly. "You could just give him a chance to prove that he's the man you want him to be, or the man you believe him to be."

Give Grant a chance. That was a thought, one I hadn't considered because of my past. "History would indicate that he's not the man I want him to be because none of them have been so far."

Shannon nodded and glanced over at her reflection to examine her roots, which were perfect because they were done by yours truly. Satisfied there were no traces of dark roots, she turned back to me. "That's the thing, Brenna, none of them work out until you find the right one. I could have kept my distance from Miles because of all the men who used me for my money, but then I would have missed out on true love, on becoming a mom and loving this crazy town."

"This isn't you and Miles."

She shrugged. "Neither were me and Miles. Until we were." That sweet loving smile that spread across her face filled me with envy.

I opened my mouth just as the bell chimed to indicate someone had entered the salon, startling me because I'd been so wrapped up in my problems I didn't notice the uniformed delivery man with the huge vase of flowers. "Hey there."

"Hey, Brenna. Got another flower delivery." The young man flashed a handsome smile that I was sure made the young girls go wild and handed over the flowers. "Lucky guy."

"Yeah, if you say so."

"I only send flowers when I really like a girl," he said with a shrug and tossed a wave over his shoulder as he left the salon.

"See? That kid is young and hot and totally full of himself, and even he sends flowers when he really likes a girl. Grant must really like you, logically speaking."

I stared at the big vase of colorful blooms, pink and purple and red and yellow and green. They were gorgeous and just staring at them brought a smile to my face. Then I read the card and felt a blush creep up my cheeks.

"Oh, what does it say? Share with the class, Ms. McKenna." Shannon's voice was filled with amusement, almost as if she knew what the card said.

"Thank you for making Mariana and her dad so happy. It's only fair I do a little something to make you happy. Grant." I stared at her with my eyebrows raised, an expression on my face that said *I told you so*. "Flowers for making Mariana happy."

"News flash Brenna, he's thanking you because it's not your job to make her happy, but you did it anyway. I won't expect Miles to come home with flowers every day because I'm being a good mom, because it's my job to be."

She made a good point. "It's so unfair, Shannon. How can I keep my distance when he does stuff like this?"

"You can stop fighting it. Don't make me get trite on you by telling you that it's better to have loved and lost than always wonder if you were too chickenshit to go after love."

Her lips twitched as she fought the laughter bubbling up inside of her.

"You need to brush up on your sayings, because I'm pretty sure you butchered that one."

Just then, the laughter exploded out of her, loud and guffawing and contagious as all get out. "My wording was more effective."

"Debatable."

"Okay, how about this one then? All is fair in love and war, or something like that. Right?" Shannon shrugged pushed out of the salon chair with a sheepish smile. "He's not playing fair, so why should you?"

Her parting words stayed with me for the rest of the day.

CHAPTER 22
GRANT

Brenna opened the door in shock, gorgeous shock. She was fresh from the shower with damp blond hair, slightly pinkened skin and a long pink robe wrapped around her body. In a word, she was mouth-watering.

"Grant. What are you doing here? Did we have plans?"

"We didn't," I told her with a smile. "But if you're not busy, I would love to whip up a little something for you. Show you my skills aren't just limited to fajitas."

Her lips quirked into a pretty smile, slightly amused. "Pretty sure you already showed me that."

"I'm glad you remember."

She fanned her face. "As if I could forget."

"Excellent." I picked the two canvas bags up, because Mariana had insisted I do my part to leave her a livable world to grow up in, and took a step forward. "So, are you busy?"

A host of emotions played across her face, each one

passing too fast to identify before the next one replaced it. Finally, she made a decision. "Not too busy to let a handsome man cook for me. Come on in."

Those were just the words I wanted to hear. "Did you have a good shower?"

She nodded and stood back to let me in, closing the door and locking it once I was inside. "It was very satisfying."

Holy shit, was she flirting with me? "I'd love to hear all about it."

Brenna's laugh was loud and throaty, full of life and amusement. She leaned on the opposite side of the counter and arched a brow. "You want me to regale you with tales of my shower?"

I nodded, pressing my luck. "Why not?"

Her blue eyes twinkled as she settled onto a stool, the movement making her robe gape just a little, offering up a tempting glimpse of soft, creamy cleavage. "Let's see, I was feeling *very* dirty after a long day at the salon, so I cranked the water as hot as I could stand it, eager to try out my new coconut pineapple body wash. Want to smell?"

I nodded and she leaned in, offering up the crook of her neck for me to inhale. "Delicious," I growled and pressed my lips to her racing pulse.

Brenna sat back, spine erect with a smile. "I lathered myself up with a good amount of soap and let the hot water rain down on my body, sliding down all the dips and curves until the water ran clear."

I licked my lips and she let out a soft, shuddering sigh.

"I lathered up twice."

"Okay." I held my hands up to get her to stop because at this point it was torture, and only the tall counter hid my state of arousal, though her smile said she already knew. "Thanks. That was very...informative."

Brenna tossed her head back, giving me a long look at the column of her neck, the way her throat moved when she laughed, the sound another thread of arousal making things below the belt painful. "What are you making?"

"My famous crispy pork chops."

"Why are they famous?"

I shrugged. "Because I say they are?"

She laughed again and pushed away from the counter. "Where's Mariana?"

Ah, now she was eager to change the subject. "With Miles and Shannon. They're babysitting."

"So it's just us for dinner?" I nodded letting my gaze settle on the sash of her robe that had loosened even further, revealing the strip of pale skin between her breasts, almost down to her belly button. "I should probably go get decent."

"Don't do it for my sake. I like the outfit you're wearing. A lot." In fact, I would prefer to see her in nothing at all, but that's not what tonight was about. Not completely anyway. I needed to show Brenna that I was here for her, not for Mariana. "A whole lot."

"Yeah?" I nodded again and licked my lips, noticing the way her eyes darkened and her pulse increased. "Then you can have it." She tossed the robe my way and disappeared down the hall, giving me a fantastic view of her heart-shaped ass as she walked away. I wanted to go after her, but the pan on the stove sizzled and smoked, reminding me that tonight wasn't just about getting Brenna out of her clothes.

"Tease!" Her laughter echoed down the hall. The sound

hit me right behind the zipper and I turned my focus to the chops and my goal of impressing her tonight.

I had a clear plan to impress her with my culinary skills, to flirt outrageously with her so there was never a doubt about how much I wanted her. To make her smile and laugh until her cheeks ached. And, if it came to it, I would show her in other, more erotic ways, just how much she meant to me.

"Dang, it smells incredible in here."

Brenna's voice pulled me from my thoughts and I turned with a smile that died on my lips. "What the hell are you wearing?"

She looked down at the royal blue scrap of silk she wore and then back up at me, eyes all wide and innocent as if she didn't know exactly what she was doing. "This? It's just a nightgown."

Just a nightgown? It was a walking hard on and she damn well knew it. "It's one hell of a nightgown." Her large breasts were pushed together and up, leaving creamy mounds for my eyes to explore while the fabric came to a stop inches above her thighs, leaving miles of leg on display just for me.

"Thanks. Beer?" Before I could tell her she was intoxicating enough, Brenna sauntered to the fridge and bent over, giving me a full view of her round ass with the smallest slip of blue fabric nestled between her cheeks. "Ale or lager?"

My eyes were glued to her ass as it swayed back and forth, tempting me to forget the meat and potatoes threatening to burn if I didn't tear my gaze away.

"Grant, ale or lager?"

"Sure, whatever." I turned towards the stove, blinking rapidly to get the vision of her ass, and all the things I wanted to do to her in that position, out of my mind. "I'm easy."

"Not tonight," she grumbled under her breath and I smiled.

"What was that?" I turned to look at her over my shoulder, smiling at her disappointed expression.

"I said ale it is." She set two bottles on the counter with more force than necessary and cracked open each bottle. "So Grant, how was your day?"

"Good. Just finished with a new group of trainees and now we're gearing up for a bunch of finance guys next week." I rolled my eyes and shook my head.

"You have a problem with finance guys?"

"No," I sighed, thrilled she was interested in knowing more about my work. "They're more bravado than action though, guys who talk a lot of smack but physically can't back it up. They don't take it so well when they fail at the obstacles and honestly, I don't know how much easier I can make them."

She shrugged and handed me one of the beer bottles. "Stop trying. If they can talk the smack, they can try harder physically. You're not some aspirin' trophy wife trying to massage their egos. Are you?"

"No."

"Then it ain't your job to make 'em feel like men. It's your job to turn them into men or help them bond or whatever, that's it. And if they get out of line, make 'em look stupid by breezing through the obstacle course without breaking a sweat. That's what I would do."

"Not sure Liam and Miles would go for that."

"Why not? You guys are all one for all, and all for one, aren't you?"

I blinked and then laughed. "You think we're The Three Musketeers?"

"A modern version of them, but yeah, pretty dang close. Am I wrong?" She blinked innocently, but the way her lips trembled told me she was messing with me. "Your skillet is smokin' again."

She was right and I reluctantly tore my gaze from her appetizing cleavage to pour a few glugs of beer into the skillet. It smoked and sizzled, which was the perfect time to pop it in the oven and set the timer. "Now, you have my full attention Brenna."

"Lucky me. First flowers and now dinner, not exactly things friends do for one another."

"We are friends, Brenna."

"I know. If we weren't friends, wearing this for dinner would be weird. Or maybe it would send the wrong signals."

"No, it's sending all the right signals. The hard peaks of your nipples pressing up against the silky fabric tells me we're on the same page. Even if one of us isn't ready to admit it yet."

"There's nothing to admit, is there? I've made no secret of my attraction to you."

"That's just physical, Brenna."

"It is," she agreed with a nod. "But isn't physical what you're after?"

I nodded. "It's not all I'm after," I assured her and walked around the counter, beer in my hand. I stopped right in front of her, gaze eating her up in that little piece of blue silk. "I'll happily lay you across the table and bring you orgasm after orgasm, with my hands and my mouth, but I'm not having sex with you tonight Brenna." The words shocked me too, but as soon as I said them, I knew it was the right way.

"Why not?"

"Because the time isn't right. When it is, you'll know."

"You sure?" She sat a little taller, the move bringing her cleavage closer to my face. My mouth.

I shook my head side to side, regret bubbling my gut. "Hell no."

She laughed. "Good to know."

I pressed a soft kiss to her lips, and I as badly as I wanted to slick my tongue across her lips before slipping inside her mouth, I took a step back. "Tell me about your day, Brenna."

She blinked, surprised but thrilled at my request. "What do you want to know?"

"That's easy. Tell me everything." I took a seat on the stool beside her, my gaze never leaving hers while I listened to her tell me about cutting and dyeing hair, listening to town gossip and making the women of Pilgrim prettier than ever.

It was the strangest date I'd had in recent memory, and I wouldn't change a damn thing about it. Not even the blue gown meant to drive me out of my mind, which it did successfully.

When I kissed her good night at the door, it took all the power I could muster to step outside and walk away.

For tonight, anyway.

Tomorrow was another matter altogether.

CHAPTER 23
BRENNA

"I'm not going back to that school and you can't make me." Mariana stood in the salon doorway with her arms folded across her little body. The dark scowl on her face lessened in impact by the lopsided pigtails she wore. "Not ever again!"

I looked up at the angry little girl and leaned on the mop I'd been using on the salon floor, and shrugged. "I have no power to make you go to school, Mariana. But you can have a seat and tell me why you're upset." I remember what it was like switching schools during the school year when cliques had already been formed and friendships bonded. It was no fun at all.

She tossed her backpack on one chair and scrambled up on another, her gaze watery as it settled back on me. "The school is doing a mommy-daughter fundraiser, and I don't have a mama. I really miss my mama, Brenna."

"I know you do, honey, and that's okay. You're allowed to miss her, and if anyone tries to tell you otherwise, you send them to me and I'll get them sorted out." My heart ached for the little girl, trying to process a grief so strong it broke most adults.

"I can't do the fundraiser without Mama." Tears fell down her cheeks in one impressive stream and I went to the little girl and gathered her in my arms.

"Your dad can do it with you. Just ask him, I happen to know that he has a hard time saying no to you."

"It's for mothers and daughters though…"

I shrugged. "Maybe, but what about little girls like you with just a daddy, or how about little girls who have two dads? They can't help the school out?"

She thought about it, long and hard, before she came up with an uncertain shrug. "I'll ask my Dad. Could you do it with me, Brenna?"

"I can, and I will if you need me, but your dad's feelings might be hurt if you don't ask him first." Grant was trying his best, and the last thing I wanted was to step on his toes.

"Okay, I will." She flashed a smile and wrapped her arms around me, squeezing tight. "Thank you, Brenna."

"That's what friends do, we talk each other down when we're acting crazy and emotional, and because we're girls, that happens a lot." I finished mopping the floor, letting Mariana sit with her feelings and process them until I was ready to take her home.

I sent a quick text to let Grant know she was with me, and prepared myself to see him again after that strange meal we shared the other night. Well, the meal itself was delicious and not at all strange, but Grant showing up to cook for me and just spend time with me without getting naked, well that was strange as hell. I still didn't get what he was trying to do, but like Shannon had suggested, I was going with it.

I decided to give him a chance to prove to me who he was, instead of deciding for myself. There was no doubt that my feelings for him hadn't just returned, they'd grown over the past weeks as I watched him step up for Mariana, and dedicate himself to being a better father and friend, a better man.

"Ready to head home, kiddo?"

Mariana nodded and followed me to my car, remaining silent the whole ride to the lake house. "Thank you Brenna, for being a good friend."

"It's my pleasure, Mari."

She wrapped her arms around my waist and squeezed. "I love you, Brenna."

"Love you too, Mariana. I promise."

Grant opened the door and found us hugging and emotional, the way women tended to be on occasion, a worried frown crinkling his eyebrows. "Everything all right?"

I stood and shook my head, nodding towards the emotional little girl. "Mari's just missin' her mama today, that's all."

He squatted down and looked her in the eyes. "Is that all, Mariana?"

She looked up at me and I gave an encouraging nod. "No. There's a mommy-daughter fundraiser at school and it just made me miss Mama." Grant pulled her in his arms and hugged her tight, the way a daddy should.

"You want to talk about her?"

She shook her head in his arms and pulled back with a

smile. "Not right now. Will you do the fundraiser with me, Dad?"

He blinked, stunned at the request. "Really? You want me to fill in for your mama?"

She nodded. "Mm-hmm."

"Then I'll be there, helping you sell...what exactly will you be selling?"

"Cookies and cupcakes and stuff. It's a bake sale."

Grant looked up at me with worry in his eyes. "Do I have to make the baked goods?"

"Duh, Dad."

"I'll help," I offered because he looked like a deer caught in headlights, and because I wanted a reason to spend more time with him.

Grant flashed a grateful smile. "Thanks. You're staying for dinner," he said, his words a command rather than a question. "I made meatballs."

"Tempting."

"And mashed potatoes. With garlic."

Garlic meant no kissing. "Sold."

He smiled as if he knew what was going through my head and took a step back, so me and Mariana could enter the lake house. "Wash your hands, girls, dinner is almost ready."

Mariana took off upstairs, leaving me to use the guest bathroom that held such wicked memories from my last visit. "Smells amazing," I moaned when I stepped into the kitchen.

"The food smells pretty good too," he growled as he stalked over and wrapped his arms around me before planting a kiss on me that vibrated through my whole body.

"Hey." His smile was bright and genuine, affection sparkled in his green eyes.

"Hey yourself."

Grant buried his face in the crook of my neck and inhaled deeply. "Coconut and pineapples, my new favorite scent combination."

I shuddered at his words, at the way his warm breath sent shivers through me.

Thankfully Mariana's feet sounded on the stairs, pulling us apart just in time before I leapt in his arms and devoured his mouth, which I fantasized about doing all through dinner. A gorgeous man who cooked and did it so well, was dangerous enough. Throw in his ability to set my body on fire while turning my legs to mush, and I was in a lot of trouble where Grant Lopez was concerned.

"I'm done, Dad. Can I go to my room?"

"You sure you're all right?" She nodded and then Grant did the same. "All right. I'll check on you in a little while."

She nodded and ran from the kitchen, tears in her eyes as she fled and I knew she was still missin' her mama.

"She'll be all right," I told him.

"I know, but it won't be easy. Sometimes the grief over my lost brothers just sneaks up on me out of nowhere, it'll knock me on my ass and it takes days before I can get back to some semblance of normal. I don't want that for her."

"I don't want that for you either, Grant, but the past is what it is. Those people are gone, and you feel that loss the same way she does." Living with grief was hard as heck but we all learned, we all adapted.

"You're right, I know." He let out a frustrated sigh that told me just how badly he wanted to take on this burden for his daughter and dammit, it only made me like him more.

"Is there anything hotter than a man telling a woman she's right?" I laughed to break up the tension and sadness.

"Yeah? Give me a minute and I'm sure I'll think of other things you were right about." He wiggled his eyebrows and I laughed. "Like that blue nightgown."

It was my turn to laugh. "That was a stroke of genius, I have to admit."

"There was a lot of stroking that night, after a very long and very cold shower." His gaze darkened, and my mind flashed with images of him in the shower, stroking his cock to thoughts of me.

"Yeah? Tell me about it." Shock registered on his face and I laughed. "Unless you want to show me?"

"Brenna," he growled. "I'm trying to be a good guy here."

I shrugged. "Who asked you to?"

"I did. I want you to see that I want you for more than your gorgeous body. I do want you, Brenna, and it has nothing to do with Mariana."

I swallowed at his words and nodded. "Wanting me makes you a bad guy?"

"No. I'm just trying to show you it's about more than that."

"Okay, fine. I guess I'll live without you putting on a show for me. For now."

He grinned and shook his head. "Go out with me, Brenna. Let me take you on a date. Dinner and dancing, the whole thing."

I wanted to say yes immediately, but I didn't. "Okay, but on one condition."

"Name it."

I sucked in a deep breath and let it out slowly. "The minute you lose interest or this stops working for you, just tell me. Don't hurt me further by trying to spare my feelings."

He blinked, stunned by my words. "Right back at you, Brenna."

I laughed and then I nodded. "Sure, I can do that. Let's just be honest about what we want and how we feel, always. Does that work for you?"

Grant nodded as he stood and strode around the table. "It more than works for me, Brenna. What I want right now is you, and what I feel is happy that you're going on a date with me, and incredibly turned on knowing that I'll have you again. Soon."

My breath hitched in my throat and I nodded. "I feel anxious and excited about our date. What I want is to go home and try out those cold showers I've been hearing so much about."

Grant laughed, and I swear it was the best damn sound I'd heard in a long time.

CHAPTER 24
GRANT

"I thought the flowers were a nice touch, but this place, it's like a first date right out of a movie." Brenna smiled across the candlelit table, a sexy little grin on her red painted lips. "Good pick, Grant."

I laughed at her plain spoken words, so typical of Brenna that sometimes I didn't know if she was making fun of me or being genuine. "Thanks, I think."

"Oh, don't let your ego betray you now, handsome, I'm being for real. This place is," she looked around the dimly lit restaurant with soft instrumental music playing in the background, giving couples plenty of privacy to talk and flirt, the long white tablecloths and the single rose that decorated each table, and smiled. "It's very romantic. Be careful Grant, I might get the wrong idea about all this." Her words were teasing, but there was a hint of fear in her voice that made me sit up a little bit taller.

"You should be careful, Brenna because I think you're finally starting to get the right idea."

She sucked in a breath and shook her head. "Grant, please."

"What? I don't know how much more obvious I can be about my intentions, Brenna. I want you. I want to spend time with you, in and out of the bedroom. I want to be the reason you smile and, my god the reason you laugh. I just can't seem to get enough of your laugh."

She smiled, sitting back in her seat with a little sigh. "Grant, you make me smile all the time."

"I know, but I want to be the main reason you smile. I want you to think about me and flash one of those big goofy grins that makes your girlfriends jealous. I want you to close your eyes and see my face, smiling at you, tasting you. Kissing you."

"Grant!" Her blue eyes went wide, and she looked around the restaurant to see if anyone was more interested in our conversation than their own. "People can hear you."

"And if they have eyes, they know damn well why I want to devour you." She'd dressed up for our date, casting off her sexy country cowgirl look in favor of a tiny red dress that had my mind focused on getting her alone and peeling that dress off her curves. "Have I mentioned how beautiful you look tonight?"

Brenna smiled and looked down, but not before I spotted the flush turning her skin a sexy shade of pink. "A time or two, but a girl never gets tired of hearing that all of her hard work is appreciated."

"Very appreciated." I lifted my tumbler of whiskey with a grin. "To you, Brenna, for giving me a deep appreciation for the appeal of cowgirl boots." She had on white boots with red tassels that I certainly wanted to see her wearing with nothing else.

"I'll definitely drink to that." She let out a soft, sexy giggle and took a long sip of bourbon. "Now that we've gotten the compliments and complications out of the way, tell me how fatherhood is treating you Grant?"

I knew what she was doing, subtly reminding me of the main reason she was on the fence about being with me, and I knew it was up to me to show her I was handling the new job of single fatherhood as well as any other single parent.

"Pretty good, actually. I mean most days I still think I'm failing her, but Mariana trusts me more with each passing day and I have to tell you, Brenna, it feels like a pretty big victory."

"Yeah? That's great to hear!"

"It feels even better to say, knowing it's true. She's starting to ask for things like a normal little girl who's confident it won't get her sent away. She's showing signs of becoming an even bigger smart ass, which is amusing and annoying."

Brenna's laugh exploded out of her, drawing a few smiles and stares from other tables. At first, she was oblivious and then she offered up apologetic smiles before turning a wide, beaming smile my way.

"You sound like a parent, Grant. Congratulations."

"Thanks. It feels good."

"I'm happy for you. Mariana is a great kid."

"She is, and even though I was terrified at first, I'm glad she's here." Mariana had changed my life in so many ways, but I didn't regret any of them. "Now if only I could convince this pretty salon owner that I want her for her crazy sayings, sexy twang, and a penchant for cowgirl boots, not to mention her sexy, husky laugh."

She let out a long sigh and smiled. "I believe you, Grant."

Her words shocked the hell out of me. "You do?"

She nodded. "Yes."

I leaned forward and took her hand in mine. "I'm going to need a little more information than that, Brenna."

She let out an amused laugh and gave my hand a squeeze. "Part of my issue is my own fears that were based on my past and had nothing to do with you. My doubts were valid, but I see now that you're not looking for a mother for Mariana."

"No, I'm looking for a woman for myself, but not just any woman, Brenna. I'm looking at you. Right at you."

"I see you, Grant. You certainly take up enough of the room." She let out a nervous laugh and shook her head. "You come off as a good time guy, but I see the SEAL and business owner in there, and the stern father that'll rise to the surface at the first curfew violation. You're formidable when you want to be."

"Damn right, I am." She licked her lips at my words and shook her head. "I've missed this, Brenna. Hanging out with you."

"Me too," she admitted quietly.

"We should do this more often, just you and me."

"And sometimes Mariana," she offered with a smile. "This was never about her, and I want you to know that, Grant. I want to be wanted for me, not my gender or my closeness with your daughter. That's all."

I nodded. "I hope I've been doing a good job of showing you that lately?"

Brenna nodded slowly. "You have and that's why I agreed to the date. At this really nice restaurant."

"You even got all dolled up for me."

"Nope, I did it for me, to make me feel more confident and comfortable on this date. I did mention you were formidable, didn't I?"

It was my turn to laugh. "You did, and it only makes me want you more, knowing how hard you find it to resist me."

"I never said you were irresistible," she insisted, her twang thicker than ever. "I said formidable."

I shrugged. "All I heard was, *Grant I find you completely irresistible. In fact, right now I'm havin' a hard time hangin' on to my panties.*"

Her face went from a blank slate to a wide grin that turned into laughter, that once again drew stares from the other diners. "Wow, I didn't realize you left the Navy due to a hearin' problem."

"It's only a problem if I'm wrong and I'm not, am I?" She swallowed, hard and dramatic, doing her damnedest to look unaffected.

"It's not a secret I find you attractive or that the chemistry between us is, off the charts."

"I think it breaks the charts, but that's just me."

"You might be right," she said with a conspiratorial smile, leaning in and reaching for her glass. Brenna took a long, torturous sip. "You might even be right about hangin' on to my panties."

"I knew it!"

"If I had any on." Her triumphant grin told me she'd been hanging on to that little nugget for the moment when it would have the most impact.

"Dammit, Brenna."

She laughed. "Is it gonna be hard, standing up to leave now that dinner's over?" She couldn't hide the laughter in her voice.

I couldn't let her win so easily. "I hear this place does magical things with chocolate cake. I heard it's got fudge and chocolate mousse between the layers of moist dark chocolate cake."

She groaned and licked her lips. "You win this round, Grant."

"I had no doubt I would."

"Just remember how much I *love* chocolate cake."

When the cake arrived, she tortured me with erotic moans for a full twenty minutes, at least twice as long as it should have taken for the small slice of cake she'd been served.

It was worth every damn minute of torture, because by the time we got to her door, I was ready to show her just how much her sexy sounds had gotten to me. "I had a great time tonight, Brenna."

"So did I." She licked her lips and took a step closer. "I really enjoyed dessert too. It's too bad you didn't want any."

"Didn't I?" It had been hard enough just watching Brenna devour that chocolate cake, there was no way I could enjoy it without smearing that frosting all over her body and licking it off. "I was hoping that I'd get my dessert a little later."

"Yeah?"

I nodded. "Yep."

She let out a sharp, throaty laugh and turned away from me. "Come on in and I'll see what I can rustle up for ya."

Brenna turned with a gleam in her eyes and took a step backwards, into her place.

I stepped inside so we were chest to chest and my presence in her space forced her to back up so her back was against the wall. "Everything I need is right here," I told her a moment before my mouth crashed down on hers, devouring her in the same way she'd devoured the cake she still tasted of. I took my time, kissing her until she shook and trembled in my arms, and then I worked my way down.

Devouring every inch of her body until she begged for her pleasure, which I happily gave her.

Twice.

CHAPTER 25
BRENNA

"I got butter, brown and white sugar, flour, sprinkles and three types of chocolate chips. What else do I need?"

"That depends on what you're making," Mara said with her usual attitude along with a heaping dose of annoyance.

"I don't know yet, but I figured it was better to have all the basics and then we can decide on specifics." I sighed in the baked goods aisle and shrugged even though I was on the phone. "How should I know? When I make cookies they're the slice and bake variety."

Shannon sighed. "Why am I even on this call? I don't bake, I manage and plan."

"Because we're friends and I need to make sure Mariana's bake sale experience is a good one. What advice do you have to offer?"

I could identify Mara's sigh by the weight of it, and I braced myself for a smart ass remark. "Just read the instructions all the way through *before* you start. Some recipes require room temperature butter and others need it very cold."

"Okay, thanks. That's helpful, Mara. Thank you."

"You're welcome. And don't screw it up because Xander supports every damn fundraiser in town, so I don't want to eat burnt or undercooked cookies with too much baking soda. Text if you have questions. I gotta go."

"Stop worrying," Shannon encouraged. "This is Grant for crying out loud. You know him and you want him, this should be fun, maybe even a little sexy."

"You're right," I sighed and grabbed a few more bags of sugar before getting in line. "Thank you, Shannon. And I'm sorry I'm such a mess about this. It's been a while since I've attempted anything like this."

"I get it. Good luck and have fun."

"Yeah, thanks." I ended the call and paid for my items before making the drive out of town to Grant's lake house. By the time I arrived, my nerves had settled some, and I was ready to do as Shannon had advised, have fun. "The cookie fairy has arrived."

Grant flashed a wide smile that I felt all the way down to my bones. "Cookie fairy? That sounds promising."

Leave it to Grant to turn it into something dirty, and leave it to my nipples to get hard as diamonds at those dirty words. "You wish."

"I do." He winked as he took the grocery bags from my hands and made his way to the kitchen. "In that white dress, you look like a sexy little country fairy."

I'd chosen a white dress that would tempt and tease him. It was lightweight cotton that was practically see-through, with three red buttons down the center of my cleavage. "This? It's my baking dress."

"Pants on fire, Brenna." There was a dark promise in his voice that I desperately wanted him to follow up on, but not now. Not today.

"Where's Mariana?" I'd started to get used to her effusive welcomes and the silent house was a little alarming.

Grant shrugged. "She's become a true kid, checking out as soon as there's work to be done. She begged to visit her friend today, and since making friends means she might stop skipping school, I said yes."

"Good decision." I'd miss her middle of the day visits, but she was a kid and she needed to be in school. "I guess you're my assistant, then?"

"Just tell me where you want me, Brenna. I am at your service.'

"Promises, promises," I teased back, feeling the room warm up at least five degrees, maybe ten. Grant leaned in close and I could read his intention all over his beautiful face as he leaned in, head slightly slanted a moment before his lips crashed down on mine.

The kiss was hotter than hell because Grant didn't take his time, he didn't warm me up, prime me for deeper more intense kisses, nope, he dove right in, licking the inside of my mouth like it was his favorite flavor on earth. His tongue licked my lips and then the seam, encouraging me to open up, and when I did, he slipped inside and kissed me until I moaned. He kissed me so deeply I had to hang on to his broad shoulders, he kissed me so hungrily I leaned into his big hard body and rubbed up against him like a cat in heat.

Grant pulled back, breathless and grinning like a fool.

"We could always buy up the supply at Bread Box and spend the evening upstairs?"

Yes, please. "You think you're the first parent who's thought of that? Mara is prepared and you won't like it, I promise you.

He dropped his forehead against mine and groaned. "So we're baking?"

"Yep, we are. But if you're a good boy, you can be dessert."

At those words, Grant stood a little taller and squared his shoulders with a wide grin. "At your service, Ms. McKenna. Anything you need."

"An apron, maybe two, to protect our clothes."

Grant tugged his t-shirt over his head and tossed it on the kitchen table before he disappeared down a short hall and returned with a checkered apron. "Done. What's next?"

I licked my lips at the sight of a shirtless Grant, smooth honey brown skin rippling with pecs and abs, and a few war wounds that served as a reminder of why he was so fit. But good lord, the man was in shape! He had muscles everywhere and each movement made one bunch and the other flex. I licked my lips again and sighed.

"Keep that up and these cookies will never get made."

"Sorry," I blinked, stealing one final glance before I pulled out my phone and searched for the recipes I'd saved last night. "Baking. We are baking cookies for a fundraiser, not getting naked for fun."

"Not yet, anyway."

"Cookies first and then nookie, maybe. *Maybe.*"

"All right," he said reluctantly and leaned forward to

steal another kiss, this one much too short to do anything but tease me. "Tell me what you need."

You. Right now. Buried deep. "You can put those muscles to good use by creaming together butter and sugar." I dumped in the amounts the recipe required and pointed at the bowl. "Mix." Grant got busy and I couldn't look away from the way his shoulders and arms bunched and flexed as he whisked the butter and sugar, making it look much easier than I knew it to be.

"I guess with Mariana around, I should learn how to bake right?"

"If you plan on this becoming a tradition, sure. My granny baked all the time, but not much for school."

"Yeah, but it's not just fundraisers like this, is it? There will be birthdays and other celebrations for when she scores her first soccer goal, makes the honor roll, or lands the lead in a school play. All of that requires congratulatory desserts, don't they?"

I stared at him for a long moment, feeling my heart race against my chest as alarm bells sounded a warning on the edges of the walls around my heart. He wasn't just looking forward to a lifetime of baking, he was planning to celebrate every event, big or small. How could a girl not fall for a guy like that?

"You are a good man, Grant. A really good man."

He set the bowl down and rolled his eyes in dramatic fashion. "That's what I've been trying to tell you, woman!"

He had been, but his actions were a much better indicator than his words. "And now I see just how good you are." He was too good to keep pushing him away, so good that another woman would snatch him up before I got my head on straight if I kept this distance between us.

"I like what I see, Grant. I like it a lot." More than I should.

"Then my evil plan is working." He winked and went back to mixing the butter and sugar, tempting me beyond all reason for the next two hours. "Hey, I think we did pretty good." Grant eyed the cookie sheets, plastic containers and cooling racks filled with cookies and cupcakes. "We make a good team."

We did. "You're an excellent assistant, maybe there's a future for you as Mara's sidekick."

"Yeah, maybe," he agreed, barely holding back a laugh. "I'm more concerned with my future with you."

"You want to be my sidekick?" I laughed, but his gaze was serious and focused on my mouth. I licked my lips and a second later, Grant's lips were on mine, attacking and devouring every inch of my lips until I submitted to his wicked kisses.

"You can call it a sidekick, but I don't think sidekicks kiss like we do. Or do other things, like we do."

"Other things?" I feigned innocence even as he pressed his bare chest against me, leaning against my side so I could feel the long thickness of his erection against my hip. "Like what?"

"Like this." He stepped right in front of me and slid one hand up the inside of my thigh, so slowly that I shuddered in anticipation, eager for him to touch me more. "You're so fucking soft, Brenna. Like silk, or maybe suede. I don't know, just soft."

I growled when his fingers brushed against the now-damp fabric of my cotton panties, back and forth, back and forth, in a hypnotic motion that made my breath hitch. "Grant."

"Yeah," he grunted in my ear. "That's exactly the sound I want to hear from that sweet mouth of yours." Before I could ask what sound he was looking for, Grant slid two fingers inside my panties and performed the same move until my knees buckled.

"Grant, please."

"Begging? Now I'm so hot, so hard for you Brenna." He didn't move, didn't take off his pants and didn't lift me up on the counter top. Instead, he found my wet center and plunged two fingers deep while his thumb worked furious circles against my clit. "What do you want, Brenna? What do you need?"

"You, Grant. Just you." It was a shocking admission, but in the throes of passion he took it to mean something else, thankfully. His lips left a trail of heat across my collarbone, kissing and licking my sensitized skin while his fingers brought me closer and closer to the edge of ecstasy. "Oh fuck, Grant! Yes!"

His hand move faster, the muscles in his forearm hard, his jaw clenched as the back of my hand brushed up and down the length of his erection. "Don't tease me, woman."

"Who's teasing?"

"Oh fuck!" The words came out on a powerful grunt as he took a step back, his green eyes dark with arousal as his fingers slipped from my body. "Taste." He held them out and I licked his forefinger and then his middle finger, swirling my tongue around each one, teasing him.

"Good."

"I thought so," he growled and dropped to his knees before he buried his face between my legs, licking and sucking me to a fast and powerful orgasm.

I let out a strangled gasp as my fingers tangled in his hair, my hips grinding the last of my orgasms out against his tongue. "Holy hell, what was that?"

"Let's call it a snack break."

My gaze narrowed. "You are one wicked man, Grant Lopez." And lord help me, but I wanted this man. I wanted him badly, and for always.

"I thought you said I was a good man?" His lips quirked into a crooked, playful smile as he licked his lips.

"You are good and wicked, or maybe you're just good at being wicked. I'll let you know when my brain is firing on all cylinders again."

He laughed. "You're damn good for my ego, Brenna."

The oven timer sounded before I could gather my wits enough for a smart ass comeback. "Cookies are done."

"Done and delicious," he said with a wicked smile and licked his lips, the move producing a shiver that went from the top of my head to the bottom of my feet. "Damned delicious."

"Wicked, wicked man."

He winked. "You love it."

I did. I really did love it, a lot.

And worse, I had a feeling I was starting to feel that word for more than his wicked ways. I was falling for the whole man.

Dang it.

CHAPTER 26
GRANT

"Ring the bell, Dad!" Mariana bounced up and down beside me, wearing an excited smile after a long day of selling cookies and cupcakes. "She's gonna be so excited, just watch."

I knocked, never taking my eyes off the little girl who'd entered my life just a few short months ago, but who I now couldn't imagine life without. "I'm not sure anyone can be more excited than you, Mari."

"Dad we sold out everything. Everything!" She stopped bouncing and grabbed my hand. "That almost never happens. I heard the other moms complaining about it. Oops, I'm not supposed to say that am I?"

"Say what?" Brenna opened the door, wearing a smile and a pair of skintight jeans that showed off her long and shapely legs.

"Hi Brenna!" Mariana flung herself at Brenna's legs, hugging with all her might. "I'm not supposed to say I was listening to adults talking about adult things."

Brenna pulled back with a curious gaze for Mari and one for me. "That depends. Did you pick up any juicy gossip? Because in this town, gossip is just as good as money."

"Really?"

I stepped in between the chattering women. "Let's not get her on the gossip train, just yet. All right?"

"Oh fine," Brenna said in a sing-song voice and stepped back. "Come on in. How did the bake sale go?"

"So good, Brenna! We sold out every cookie and every cupcake you made! Every single one of them, how cool is that?"

"Very cool. I'm sure it had more to do with your adorable self than my cookies."

"No way, everyone loved the chocolate chunk cookies so much. Even dad bought a dozen just for us. Lots of moms bought the skinny sugar cookies too."

"I'll just bet they did," she said, her blue eyes lit with mischief as they landed on me. "Congratulations then, on a successful day."

"We're taking you out to dinner," Mariana proclaimed. "As a thank you and because I missed you."

"Pizza?" Mariana nodded. "I do love pizza."

"Me too," she said with an excited jump.

"I do too," I added with a sardonic grin. "Not that anyone asks."

"You're a boy, Dad, of course you love pizza." She turned back to Brenna. "So you'll come to dinner with us?"

"Absolutely. It's important to celebrate every win, big or small."

Her smile brightened. "That's what Mama always said too. I have to use the bathroom."

"Down the hall on the right," Brenna said with laughter in her voice. "She's in a good mood."

"I am too. Now." I stepped in and cupped her face, kissing her slowly and gently, tasting every inch of her mouth because I simply could not get enough of this woman. "Hi."

"Well, hey there, handsome. Long day?"

I nodded. "The longest. It was an endless line of single moms flirting and pressing their tits in my face."

"Sounds like a good time for a young, virile man."

"Normally it would've been, but I could only think about one woman and one set of boobs."

She let out a throat laugh and pressed another kiss to my lips. "You're only thinkin' about me because I did that thing you like."

I grunted and pressed my body against hers. "Don't talk about it or I won't be able to control myself." All day, flashes of those bright red lips wrapped around my cock, haunted me. Tortured me. It was the longest, slowest blow job of my life and produced an orgasm so powerful I fell to my knees. "See what you've done?"

She pressed against me and laughed. "Tempting. But there's a little girl down the hall and pizza for dinner."

"Tease," I growled and nipped her ear.

"You love it," she shot back with a teasing grin but the truth was I did love it, and I had a sinking feeling I was starting to love the woman too.

"Okay, I'm ready!" Mariana's quick footsteps sounded until she came to a skidding stop right in front of us. "I want cheeseburger pizza, please."

"You heard the girl." Brenna arched her blond brows into a teasing expression. "Let's go get pizza!"

We made quick time on the walk over to the pizza parlor, with Mariana keeping up a steady conversation along the way. Watching the two females together, so animated and happy to just be around each other, was a revelation. It made me start to think of things I wasn't sure I should be thinking, things I wasn't honestly sure I was even ready to think about. But the way Brenna took Mariana by the arm and twirled her in dancing circles while they waited for a couple of cars to pass, had me second-guessing my own thoughts and wants and feelings.

The restaurant was packed with families. And loud. We were seated at a table right in the middle of the chaos, which I didn't mind, except we drew stares from all directions. Which I did mind.

"Cheeseburger pizza, please!"

Brenna laughed. "Gotta love a girl with a one track mind." Her laugh drew a few looks, as it always did, and she was, of course, completely unaware of her effect on people. "How do you feel about Italian sausage and peppers?"

"Sounds good to me," I told her and placed the orders.

"So, did anything else interesting happen at the bake sale today?" Mischief twinkled in her eyes and I wondered if she'd heard something, not that there was anything worth hearing.

"One of the mothers thought she could pass off Mara's confections as her own."

Her blue eyes went wide. "Oh no!"

"Exactly," I laughed. "It wasn't until the last minute that

she realized Mara had added 'made by Mara' on the bottom of each cupcake. In red gel frosting."

"Oh. My." Before she could finish the sentiment, Brenna erupted in laughter. Her shoulders shook and her cleavage jiggled in a mouthwatering fashion. She made a beautiful picture and I couldn't take my eyes off of her. "Classic Mara, but ouch, brutal."

I laughed at her correct assessment. "She was pretty embarrassed but they sold out and that's what matters, at least that's what I told her."

"And how did that work out for you?"

"Let's just say she found me a lot less appealing after that."

Brenna gasped and put a hand to her chest in mock outrage. "Now that I don't believe."

"Believe it, babe." I winked and she rolled her eyes, but the smile on her full lips told me she appreciated it.

"Well isn't this a cozy scene?"

I didn't recognize the voice but the woman had a baby on one hip and a kid about Mariana's age bouncing at her side, pegging her as one of the school mothers. "It is, thanks. Can I help you?"

The woman huffed out a laugh. "You don't remember me, do you?"

"Should I?" I knew I hadn't dated her because in the past I stayed away from single moms because there was too much expectation. "Your kid goes to school with my daughter, right?" I looked to the game room where Mariana laughed with friends, wishing she was here to tell me who the hell this woman was.

"Yeah. I gave you my number and you never called. Now

I know why." She glared at Brenna. "So you two are together, huh?"

"How is that any of your business?" Brenna's thick accent was loud and now half the restaurant had tuned in. "All you need to know is that he didn't call. Honestly!"

"I just want to know if I'm barking up the wrong tree. No need to get catty about it." She hoisted the kid higher on her hip, still glaring at Brenna.

"Not catty, just telling you to mind your business, which *my* business is not."

Thankfully our teenage waiter chose that moment to arrive with our drinks and food. He carefully nudged the woman out of the to set down to hot pizzas. "Do you need more chairs?"

"No thanks, honey. She was just leaving." Brenna glared at her with a serene smile on her face until the woman growled and stomped off. "What a hot commodity you are. Should I feel honored or somethin'?"

I laughed. "Or something, yeah." We stared at each other for several long moments, heat arcing between us, unspoken passion stoking the flames.

"Yay, pizza!"

Brenna's lips curled into an amused grin as she turned her attention to Mariana. "It's like you have a radar for pizza, little girl."

"I do. I think. What's a radar?"

Brenna laughed again. "It means you have an extra sense to know when there's pizza around."

"Oh." Mariana's shoulders relax. "Yeah I have that 'cause I *love* pizza."

"Then let's protect our clothes before we dig in."

"I'm too big for a bib," Mariana insisted and I couldn't help but grin.

"First of all, you're never too big for a bib because you can eat as messy as you want, but this is pizza so we'll just use a napkin." Brenna showed her how to fold the napkin and tucked into the collar of her shirt to keep it pizza sauce free. "Easy peasy."

"Lemon squeezy," Mariana added with a giggle.

The longer the meal went on, the more I started to see Brenna in my life. In *our* lives.

By the time we said goodnight on Brenna's doorstep, I realized that somewhere along the way, I fell for Brenna McKenna.

CHAPTER 27
BRENNA

"Oh, for crying out loud, Brenna, just tell the man how you feel!" Jessie May's words vibrated with affection and frustration, her emotions were palpable over the phone.

I sighed and shook my head before burying it in my hands. "That's just it, Jessie May, I'm not totally sure how I feel!"

"Liar." Her accusation was softened by the mocking laughter that sounded from her end, at least a little.

"I'm not lying, I swear. I like Grant, a lot. Probably a lot more than I should, but that doesn't make this love, Jessie. It could be delirium brought on my amazing orgasms. It could be nothing more than a crush, or worse, infatuation."

"Even you don't believe that, Brenna. All I'm saying is that you'll have to stop running from love at some point."

"First of all, I'm not running. I'm simply exercising a bit of caution." That was my story and I planned on sticking to it. Grant emotionally confused me. At dinner the other night, I caught him staring at me with a strange expression on his face. It was close to love, maybe just pure affection, but he looked like a man who cared. Who *more* than cared.

Yet he said nothing.

"There's caution, Brenna, which is smart. But what you're doing is avoiding even having the talk. Just spit the words out and see what happens. Maybe Grant will surprise you."

I wanted to believe that, but I couldn't. Luckily, my first customers of the day walked in and provided the perfect distraction. "Gotta go, Jessie May, there's work to be done. Love you."

"Good luck. Let me know how it goes."

The call ended and I lost myself in the dance of my work, shampooing and dyeing hair, clipping split ends, setting dozens of curlers and styling until my fingers cramped. It was a busy day, filled with female camaraderie, gossip and more customers than I knew what to do with.

It was exactly the kind of a day a small business owner in a small town hoped to have. A couple days like this every month and I could stop stressing so much about my business.

By lunchtime the place was empty again, giving me time to refill, disinfect and sweep. There was always sweeping to be done, so much sweeping I rarely had to worry about how my arms looked in a tank top, another bonus of the job. At least that's what I told myself each time I reached for the broom, which happened at least twenty times a day.

The phone rang and I sighed with relief at the reprieve from the sweeping. "Hello?"

"Brenna?"

The voice was small and quiet but I could still hear her tears. "Mariana? Honey, what's wrong?" I took it as a win that she hadn't left school grounds and run straight to the salon, but that only intensified my worry. "Mari, talk to me."

"I don't feel good, Brenna. I got sick and the school nurse thinks it's an allergy but she can't get my dad on the phone." The little girl dissolved in tears, which was a testament of how truly awful she felt.

"Put the nurse on the phone, please."

"This is Nurse Johnson. Ms. McKenna?"

"Yes, that's me. Do you need me to run out to bodyguard school and get Grant to the school? I'm happy to do it."

"That would be great but it might be more prudent for you to come and get her since word around Pilgrim is that you guys are dating."

Word around town? "That's news to me and I don't remember Grant putting me on the list as an approved adult to pick up his daughter."

"He hasn't even though the principal told him a few times he needed a backup, but this is a small town Ms. McKenna and Mariana needs you."

"Call me Brenna," I told her as my gaze scanned the salon to double-check everything was safe for me to leave for a few hours. "I need to close up the salon and then I'll be there."

"Thank you, Brenna."

"No problem." I locked up the salon, calling Grant twice as I made my way to the car, and getting no answer. I tried calling him again before I went inside the school to pick up Mariana. "Grant, it's Brenna. Call me back right away."

"Brenna!" Mariana's skin was pale and her voice was quieter than usual, even her hug didn't hold the same energy as normal. "You came."

"Of course, I did. You needed me so I'm right here. Ready to go?"

She nodded. "Do I have to go to the hospital?"

I nodded. "Yep. That's where the experts are and they'll know exactly how to make you feel better." It was the last place I wanted to go but this wasn't about me, it was about a child. "Come on, honey."

The silent car ride was another sign that Mariana was still feeling awful, but when the questions began, I couldn't help but smile. "Are you and my dad dating, Brenna?"

"Yes, I think. Maybe. Sort of." It wasn't exactly a clear answer, then again I didn't exactly have a clear idea what was actually going on between me and Grant.

"It's okay with me if you guys are dating. I love you, Brenna."

I reached out and put my hand on her shoulder, giving it a small squeeze. "I love you too, Mari."

"You do?" I nodded. "If you guys stop dating, will you still be my friend?" The worry in her voice was too much for a girl her age and it broke my heart.

"I will always be your friend, Mariana. Always."

"Good." She let out a small yawn and snuggled deeper into the seat, the barest hint of a small on her pale lips.

When we arrived at the hospital, I felt like a fish out of water, not the least of which because Mariana wasn't my kid, but because I couldn't answer any of the intake questions and Grant still hadn't answered his phone. "Dammit,

Grant. Where are you?" Mariana was curled up beside me in one of the hard plastic chairs, half asleep. "Luna! She'll have answers."

She didn't answer either so I left an urgent message to call me back and turned my attention back to Mariana, whose groaning had increased considerably. Another good thing about small town living was that the staff didn't stand on ceremony when it came to treating sick kids.

"All right, Munchkin, let's get you into the exam room." I got the little girl situated on the exam table and kept my hand in hers while the nurse took her vitals.

"We need to take a peek inside your throat now, Mariana. Is that okay?" The nurse flashed a kind smile and Mari nodded. Fifteen seconds later, Mariana struggled to breathe, her little limbs flailed frantically and I covered her little body with mine.

"Stop. We have to stop." I looked in horror at Mari's swollen, pale face and let out a sharp cry of surprise. "What in the hell?"

Just then I got a text message from Luna. "Allergic to cantaloupe and latex."

"Shit. She's allergic to latex."

The nurse jumped back like she was coated in acid and stripped off the gloves, shoving them deep in the biohazard bin before ordering something to stop the allergic reaction. Two minutes later, Mari was calm—sort of—and the nurse wore some other type of gloves that caused no tears and no swelling. "All right, champ. Sorry about that but you did very good, Mariana. We'll have your results soon."

Alone again, I sat on the bed and wrapped my arms

around a still sniffling Mariana and rocked her until she was calm again.

"Where in the hell do you get off?" Grant's loud bellow scared the crap out of me and Mariana.

I pulled away from the little girl and rubbed her back. "Grant."

"Well? Answer me." He stood there, cutting an imposing figure with his arms crossed, his jaws clenched tight and fire bursting out of his eyes. He was angry but the truth was that he was scared, but in true macho man style, he refused to show any hint of vulnerability.

I sighed because there was nothing I could say to penetrate his anger or his fear in the moment. So, I went for a basic explanation. "The school called me because of gossip and since you weren't answering your phone, I figured it was more important to get Mariana help. Period."

"And you thought it was your place to get her to the hospital? She's not even your damn kid!"

Ouch. His words hit me like a blow to the chest and I felt my skin turn to ice. "Right." Nodding absently, I turned back to Mariana and dropped a kiss on her forehead. "Love you, little girl. Feel better." With a heavy heart and tears in my eyes, I avoided Grant's gaze as I slipped out of the hospital room.

"Brenna, come back!"

I didn't respond or acknowledge I'd heard his anguished plea, instead I walked faster until I was in the safety of my car. I was done with Grant.

Completely done.

I should have listened to my instincts, because they were

never wrong. If I cared about a man then there was something wrong with him, always. Without a doubt.

Well that was a mistake I refused to make again. My last thought as the hospital faded from my view, was that I was glad I hadn't told Grant how I felt about him.

Because right now, I hated him.

CHAPTER 28
GRANT

"You have reached Brenna and I am super busy and important." I ended the call because I couldn't stand to listen to her chipper voice mail message for the fiftieth time in three days. Three damn days. She never picked up the phone when I called and she didn't respond to any attempts to reach her by text message. "This is ridiculous."

"Problem?" Liam and Mason stood in the doorway of my office, doing a piss poor job of hiding their glee at my frustration.

"Damn right I have a problem. Brenna hasn't responded. At all. Nothing but radio silence." I knew I was a dick to her, knew it in the moment but my fear over Mariana had overridden all of that. "Is that all it takes for a woman to be done with you, one mistake?"

AT those words, my friends collapsed in laughter. "You haven't even apologized yet, so it's a little soon for you to be playing the victim, don't you think?" Miles' tone took the sting off his words but I wasn't deterred.

"How can I apologize when she won't answer the damn phone?"

"I know," Liam agreed with a shake of his head. "Pilgrim is huge, it would be impossible to find her in this vast metropolis."

He wasn't wrong, but I had my reasons. Mostly those reasons were that I was a coward and I didn't want to face Brenna's wrath in person because I was such a monumental prick to her when she was only trying to help. "Mariana isn't talking to me either."

Miles laughs. "Women stick together, my friend. Shannon wants to cut your man parts off, if that makes you feel any better."

"How is that supposed to make me feel better?"

He shrugged. "It's not just your kid who's pissed at you, I guess."

"Yeah, that doesn't help at all, but thanks Miles." I let out a frustrated sigh and sat back in my chair. "I was just scared and I completely overreacted, and Brenna was the closest target."

"But then you went too far," Liam reminded me as if I needed the damn reminder.

"Yeah," I agreed. "You guys suck at making me feel better."

"You're lucky I'm here at all. Olive told me to kick you in the nuts," Liam said with a smile. "I haven't completely ruled it out. Yet."

"Thanks."

"Anytime." Liam flashed a menacing smile as he

smacked his hands together. "So, what are you gonna do, just sit here and bitch about it all day?"

Liam was right in his own gruff way. "No. Hell no." I stood and started to pace the length of my office to get my thoughts together. "No," I said again and stopped to stare at my friends. "I have to go."

"Finally found his balls," Liam said with a loud, boisterous laugh. "Good luck."

"Yeah, thanks," I grumbled and made my way to my car and into Pilgrim. I found an open parking spot which I took as a good sign, at least until I arrived at Brenna's salon. The place fell silent and I didn't know if it was because a man had invaded their sacred space, or if everyone knew what a prick I'd been to their favorite salon owner. "Is Brenna here?"

"Nope. She's not here." The dark haired woman who answered me I had hair clip in her mouth and several more stuck to her smock, and worse, she seemed completely uninterested in helping me.

"Do you know where she is or when she'll be back?" I was desperate for any kind of information on Brenna. Three days was too long go to without her smile, without her laugh and her quirky country sayings.

"Yes I know where she is and no, I don't know when she'll be back." The woman turned back to the customer in her chair and sighed. "Have a good day."

After spending years in the military, I knew a dismissal when I heard one. "Thanks." For nothing.

"You betcha!"

The sound of more than a dozen women laughing carried me out of the salon, feeling annoyed and dejected. It didn't matter if they knew what I'd said to Brenna, all that mattered was that she wanted away from me bad enough that she was hiding from me.

Hiding.

From me.

Instead of going back to the office, I made my way home, hoping that I could at least fix things with Mariana. "Mari!"

"She's in her room." The older woman, Rosie, I hired to watch Mariana after school flashed a soft, sympathetic smile.

Of course she was, because she spent every waking minute in her room since I brought her home from the hospital. "Isn't she too young to be acting like a teenager already?"

Rosie laughed. "They're always too young, Grant." She gave my shoulder a sympathetic pat and then shuffled towards the door. "Be patient with her."

"I will be. Thank you, Rosie."

"See you tomorrow," she sang and closed the door behind her with a soft click.

"Mari, I brought ingredients for nachos!" There was a long silence and I thought she would leave me hanging again, but a full minute later, her small footsteps sounded on the stairs.

"Nachos?"

"Yep." I turned with a wide smile at her quiet voice. "I got beef and beans and corn, avocados, cheesy tortilla chips, sour cream. Pretty much I got all the fixings so we can make them however we want them."

Mariana gave the ingredients a bored onceover and shrugged. "Okay."

It wasn't the exuberance I was used to, but it was progress and I accepted it. We worked together in silence until the table was laden with all the ingredients necessary for nachos. "This is quite a spread, don't you think?"

"It's a lotta stuff." Her words were meant to be nonchalant but the way her eyes widened in lowkey giddiness told me I hadn't lost her completely. Not yet.

"Ready to eat?"

"Yes!" Mariana climbed into her chair and got busy piling a little bit of everything on top of her nachos until the pile was taller than her. "Yum."

"You can always come back for more, kiddo," I told her with an indulgent smile. "How was school today?"

"Fine."

Fine. It had taken weeks to even get her to stay in school for a full day, and longer than that before she had anything kind to say about school, the students or the teachers. And now we were back to fine. "Did you learn anything new today?"

She sighed. "We learn stuff every day."

I worked really hard to hide my frustration as a father but it was a long day. "You can't stay mad at me forever, Mariana."

"I know but you were mean and you hurt Brenna's feelings."

"I know." Getting dressed down by your seven year old kid would be a humbling experience for any man, but when combined with that admonishing stare, I felt myself wilt. "I was awful to her, Mari, I know that. I've been trying to find her to apologize and find some way to make it right."

"She's visiting her sister, Jessie May."

I blinked that the first real news of Brenna was coming from my daughter. "How do you know?"

"Because, Dad, I made her promise that we would still be friends if you two broke up, which you did. That's how I know!" With those parting words, Mariana pushed away from the table and her half-eaten pile of nachos and stomped her way back up the stairs, punctuating her feelings with every stomp of her little feet.

Left alone with my thoughts and my dinner, I let my misery sink in and wrap around me like a blanket because it's no less than what I deserve.

Eventually I got up my nerves and reached for my phone, saying exactly what I should have said days ago. "I'm sorry."

CHAPTER 29
BRENNA

"I'm sorry." I rolled my eyes at the message from Grant. I'll just bet he was sorry now, because screwing up in a small town could make for a difficult life.

"You'll have to answer him at some point," Jessie May said the words in a sing-song voice that brought a smile to my face.

I shook my head. "You see, Jessie, that's the beauty of a casual relationship. It's casual so there is no need for a big breakup scene or a post breakup talk. You can just stop reaching out to each other, stop calling and that's it, casual thing over." I snapped my finger. "Just like that."

Jessie May rolled her eyes and let out the world's most dramatic sigh. "Except you guys aren't over and you know it. He was scared and he lashed out. Horribly, yes, but you know it wasn't about you."

"See Jessie May, that's the thing, you can lash out at your husband, your best friends, your siblings because those relationships are long and deep, they can handle it. You don't get to just lash out at some girl you're casually hanging out and hooking up with. He doesn't get to have it both ways. He doesn't."

"That's fair," she finally conceded. "But that doesn't mean you guys are done. This is just one of those little hurdles on your way to happily ever after."

I rolled my eyes and groaned. "Pregnancy hormones are turning you into a lovesick fool. Emphasis on fool."

Jessie May held her growing baby bump and laughed. "What can I say, I love, love and I really love romance!" Her feminine giggles made it impossible to stay upset and I just rolled my eyes.

"You are ridiculous, but I love you anyway."

"And you love Grant too. The sooner you can admit it, the better everything will be."

I shook my head and ignored two more text messages from Grant. "Things are fine, Jessie May. Just fine."

"So fine that you ran all the way to Louisiana to lick your wounds?"

"Yeah. Obviously. That's what family is for, right?"

"Yep, and for giving you a hard time. It's my god given right." Her toothy grin was contagious and I laughed.

"Which you've successfully done, for days now. Thank you, Jessie."

"My pleasure, honey."

Two days and another half dozen text messages later, my plane landed back in Texas and I took my time navigating the huge parking lot to find my car. I was ready to be back at home, more importantly, I was ready to be back at the salon.

The one thing I sure as hell was *not* ready for, was to see six feet of hot, well-muscled man leaning against my car, wearing a disarming smile. "Brenna. Hi."

"Grant." His name came out on a snort and I shook my head as I rounded the vehicle to toss my suitcase into the trunk. "I can do it," I insisted when he easily lifted the suitcase from my hands.

"I just want to help, Brenna."

"Yeah, well who asked for your help? In fact, what the hell are you even doing here?"

He blinked, as if shocked by the question. "I'm here for you."

"Why?"

"Seriously? Because I've been trying to reach out to you for days without any response from you."

"Some men might take the hint."

His deep chuckle sounded right beside me as I finally managed to get the oversized suitcase in the trunk. "Some men are too easily scared at the sight of an angry woman."

"Angry. Who's angry?"

"You are," he whispered in my ear. "And you have every damn right to be angry."

"Gee, thanks," I offered with a derisive snort. I frowned at the sight of Grant standing on the other side of my car. "What do you think you're doing?"

He grinned as if this was some kind of game and shoved his hands deep in his pockets. "Think I can get a ride back to Pilgrim with you?"

A ride. Back to Pilgrim. "Whatever," I muttered more to my self than to Grant. "And stop smiling about it."

His smile didn't dim even a little. "Yes ma'am."

The first hour of the drive was made in tense silence, which I didn't mind all that much since it was difficult enough just being stuck in my small sedan with Grant's big body and his oversized presence.

"How was your visit with Jessie May?"

"Fine."

"Mariana finally put me out of my misery and told me you were visiting your sister." He let out a huff of laughter and I could see him shaking his head. "I thought it meant she was finally starting to forgive me."

Curiosity got the better of me. "It didn't?"

"Hell no," he laughed. "Told me how she made you promise you'd be friends forever, no matter what happened between us, and then she reminded me what a big fat jerk I was before leaving me alone at the dinner table."

I couldn't help but smile at that because the little girl was growing up to be quite a spitfire. "She's comfortable enough with you to be mad, that's a good sign." And I was happy for him. For both of them, actually.

"That's what I keep telling myself, Brenna."

I ignored the way my name rolled off his tongue and the shiver it produced. He didn't deserve my sympathy or anything else.

"I'm sorry, Brenna."

I raised a hand up to stop his words. "We don't really need to do this Grant. It's unnecessary."

He growled. "Unnecessary because you're not mad at me anymore?"

"Unnecessary because I knew what you were doing and why, at the time."

"You did? So what's with the radio silence?" His outrage was palpable and I refused to be affected by that.

"Grant, all you wanted was something casual and that was working great for us, but the way you lashed out at me, that's not how you treat a casual partner."

"I know. That's why I'm sorry." He raked a hand through his hair and let out a long, slow sigh. "I shouldn't have said any of what I said to you."

"You think?" My sarcasm was thick because his apology wasn't sincere. "You hurt me Grant and that's what you should be sorry for."

"I know-,"

"No, Grant, you don't know. You think I don't know Mariana isn't my daughter? Because I held her on the way to the hospital and tried, in vain, to answer the intake questions about her health history. That made it pretty clear who I am to her, just a friend. But that didn't change how scared I was for her *as if* she were my kid. You were too busy to pick up your phone and I was happy to step in and help you, and that's how you repay me, by hurting my feelings."

"That wasn't my intention, Brenna, you have to know that."

"Maybe not but that's what happened."

"What does that mean for us?"

"It means your actions showed me exactly how important I am to you, Grant."

"Obviously not because you are important to me, Brenna. So damn important."

"No Grant, you like having sex with me and that's fine, because I liked having sex with you too. But this thing we're doing has reached its inevitable conclusion." To punctuate my point, I pulled into his driveway and waited for him to get the hell out of my car.

He did but not without one final parting shot. "This isn't over, Brenna."

I didn't bother responding because it was over, Grant just hadn't realized it yet. With tears in my eyes, I made my way to my empty house where I didn't even have a pet to greet me, and found a very pregnant Shannon waiting on my porch with cupcakes and bourbon. "Wanna talk about it?"

"Nope, because there's nothing to talk about. But I am hungry for cupcakes and thirsty for bourbon. I might even have sweet tea for you and the baby." Because at the end of the day, all a girl needed was her friends.

CHAPTER 30
GRANT

"So you struck out, huh?" The sympathy in Liam's words took the sting out of his question.

"It was worse than striking out. I'm pretty sure that waiting like I did just gave her more time to get used to living without me." I shook my head in disgust and anger. "I don't know who that angry, cold woman was because it wasn't Brenna. Not my Brenna, anyway."

Miles nodded and crossed one leg over his knee, posed in a thoughtful position. "Tell us exactly what she said."

I gave the guys a blow-by-blow of the eternal car ride home with Brenna, ending with me telling her it wasn't over yet. "She didn't even respond to that, just peeled out of the driveway as soon as I closed the door behind me."

"She sounds proper pissed," Liam offered up. "It's time to go big, my friend, or get off the pot."

Miles laughed. "I think you're mixing metaphors."

"He knows what I mean, don't you Grant."

I nodded because I had been thinking the same thing. "It means it's time for a grand gesture. Any ideas?"

"Yeah, skip the big gestures and just tell Brenna how you feel about her." Miles' no nonsense words were out of character and I looked up at him with a frown.

"I already tried that and she didn't want to hear it."

"No, man. None of this I care about you crap, tell her you love her. Tell her that she means the world to you and you can't imagine loving another woman the way you love her."

"That's good stuff," Liam insisted with a grin. "Listen to Miles."

It was good, those words of his, but you couldn't just poach a man's words of love and repeat them to a woman, could you? "So I shouldn't do a big gesture?"

Miles sighed. "You need to do something that will mean something to Brenna."

I spent the rest of the day trying to figure out exactly what I needed to do in order to win Brenna back. Was *back* even the right word? She'd as much as admitted that we were nothing more than a casual fling, which meant I had a few hurdles to clear.

I thought about starting with flowers but that seemed too cliché, then again cliches *were* cliches for a reason and that was because they worked. Flowers were too obvious and she would probably just dump them in the trash or give them to one of her gray-haired clients.

But there was one thing in this town that I knew Brenna would find completely irresistible, Bread Box. I made my way over and just outside the doors, I prepared myself for Mara's wrath.

"Next!"

I stepped forward, palms sweating and heart racing. "I'd like a dozen of Brenna's favorites."

"A dozen? I guess the rumors are true, you stepped in it big time."

"Yeah, I did. And this is step one on the road to redemption."

Mara grinned. "My pastries are good, but I'm not sure I put any redemptive qualities in any of them. Sorry," she said not looking sorry at all.

"Then I guess I better come up with something witty and heartfelt to say to make that redemption happen."

"Excellent idea, because as good as these pastries are, and they are damn good, you'll need more."

"I know. And I have a plan for that." It was a little bit sneaky and yeah, a little underhanded too. But when you screwed up the way I did, you had to go big.

And now, armed with a dozen pastries, I had a plan.

CHAPTER 31
BRENNA

"You got a special delivery!" Mariana's voice rang out above the chaos of the salon and I turned with a smile for the little girl.

"Yeah? Who has a special delivery?"

"You do, Brenna!" She jumped with the same level of excitement she reserved for ice cream, pizza and sleepovers. Mariana took in a deep breath to calm herself and then she slowly walked over to me. "This is for you, Brenna."

I accepted the small but familiar pastry box with a smile. "This is for me? Thank you, Mari."

"It's from my Dad," she said proudly and the entire salon went up in a chorus of awww.

"Well open it up, Brenna! We all want to see what her dad sent to you."

I opened up the pastry box and smiled at the oversized red velvet cupcake. "Red velvet."

"Oh, Mara is a genius when it comes to red velvet," someone called out and I nodded absently.

My attention was focused on the small ribbon of paper inside the box. "Your laughter is my favorite sound in the world." Damn, Grant was good. Really good. The question was, did one little pastry and a really great compliment mean forgiveness?

No. No it did not.

"Well, what do ya think Brenna?" Mariana looked up at me with wide, curious eyes, a smile teasing her lips.

I broke the cupcake in half and gave her part of it. "This is delicious. Be sure to thank your dad for me."

"You could thank him yourself when he comes to pick me up. Soon." She looked at her watch-less wrist and grinned. "Soon."

The little girl was trying to help matchmake her daddy. It was sweet. And low. "As nice as that sounds, this place is packed and I have to get back to work." And if I could manage to be searching for some obscure hair product when Grant arrived to pick up Mariana, that would perfect.

Just perfect.

I swear the whole dang town was in on the game because Grant's truck made an appearance about fifteen seconds after the last customer gave a knowing smile and wave as she exited the salon. "You gonna be mad at my dad forever, Brenna?" Nothing cut like the innocently spoken question from a child.

"I'm not mad at him, Mari, not anymore." I was just done with him, needed to be for my own peace of mind.

"You just don't want him?"

I looked up just in time to see Grant's lazy sexy gait strolling up to the shop, a nervous smile on his face. "That question is a little too grown up for you, Mariana."

"I knew you were gonna say that," she grumbled adorably just as the chimes sounded over the door. "Dad!"

"Hey baby girl! Did you have a good day?" Mariana gave an exaggerated nod as she wrapped her arms around Grant and I couldn't help but take in the scene with a heavy heart because, no matter how much I tried to fool myself, to lie to myself, I'd started to see this little family as mine. "That's good. Really good to hear." Grant smacked a kiss on both cheeks and the little girl giggled.

"Brenna loved the cupcake and she shared it with me." Her stage whisper could use some work, but some things were just too exciting for a little girl of seven years to keep it quiet.

"Even better news." Grant stood and dusted imaginary debris from his pants before turning his gaze to me. "Looking gorgeous, as always, Brenna."

Yeah, I smiled. I couldn't help it because the man was charming as all get out. "Thanks, Grant. Charming as ever, I see."

"Is it working?"

I shrugged. "The cupcake was delicious. The message was...received."

"Perfect." He flashed that picture perfect smile, his gaze lingering on my face for a seconds longer than might be considered appropriate, before he dropped down to his knees and ordered Mariana up on his back. "Let's let Brenna get back to work. See you soon, Brenna." His words sounded more like a threat than a promise and I worked hard to suppress a shiver.

"Bye, Brenna."

And that was it. Grant and his matchmaking partner were gone.

Weird.

It was kind of a letdown but I shoved that thought deep down into a box, wrapped it in chains and locks, and promptly forgot about it. This was good. I didn't Grant trying to seduce me, or woo me or whatever that sweet note had been.

It was a relief, actually.

Yeah, a relief, that's what it was.

At least, that's what I told myself as I clipped and dyed and set hair for the rest of the afternoon, determined not to spend the whole day thinking about how things had gone so terribly wrong with Grant Lopez. The truth was things hadn't gone wrong, per se, I'd just fallen for the wrong guy.

Again.

But the thing about Grant Lopez was, he didn't feel like the wrong guy and that's what made him so dangerous. Which I was reminded of once again when I stepped inside my house later that day and found every surface filled with flowers and chocolates and plenty of other things that made me wonder what the heck he was up to. "Hello?" There was no answer. Of course there was no answer because the house was empty. But I grabbed for my bat just to be sure. "I'm armed so if you value the brains in your head, make yourself known. Now." It was a ridiculous thing to say to someone who had broken into your home to hand out gifts, but it was all I had.

"Well now, that's not the greeting I was hoping for but it's so quintessentially Brenna that I'll take it."

Grant. "How did you get in here?"

His brows arched in question. "I have a particular set of skills."

I held my hands up to stop his words with a smile. "Nope. We're not doing that."

"Okay fine. I got by with a little help from my friends. Better?"

I nodded, feeling a little swoony that he'd recruited his friends to help him pull this off, whatever *this* was. That had to mean something. Didn't it? "Some. What is all this?"

"Look around and see for yourself."

I accepted his challenge and went around the living room with a hitch in my throat. The first one I came upon was a lemon cheesecake bite and a little paper ribbon that said *your smile is the best part of my day.* "Grant," I gasped.

"What can I say, darlin'? When I'm around you, I aspire to be the funniest man in the world just so I can see your smile and hear your laugh. It's intoxicating."

I felt my cheeks flame at his words and moved on. Next was an oversized mint chocolate chip cookie beside a familiar shoe box with a note attached. *There's no such thing as too many boots for the perfect cowgirl.* Inside the box were a gorgeous pair of elaborately decorated cowboy boots, the good kind that would still carry you on the dance floor in twenty years. I turned to Grant with a shaky smile. "These are lovely."

Grant ambled over to where I stood and snagged the cookie with a smile. "The perfect excuse to spend the rest of our lives twirling you around the dance floor."

The rest of our lives? "What?"

His deep laugh sounded. "I've shocked you."

"Uh, yeah. A little."

"Then let me be clear, Brenna. I was fooling myself to think we could ever be anything close to casual. You're a good time, that's for damn sure, but you're the kind of woman that once a man gets his hands on her, gets a taste of her, she's all he can think about. You're all I think about. You are what I crave, Bren."

"Grant."

"I've fallen for you Brenna. There is no other way to explain this upside down, don't know whether I'm coming or going sensation you create whenever you're around. I'm in love. With you."

"With me?"

His lips twitched with barely leashed laughter. "I am in love with you, Brenna McKenna."

I sucked in a sharp breath of surprise at his words even as my shoulders relaxed and my heart rate doubled in intensity and speed. "Oh Grant, I love you too."

"You do? Thank god, woman!" He pulled me close and wrapped his arms tight around me. "Are you sure, because I have a big speech prepared about how I would give you as much time as you need to come around and love me too."

"I don't need it, Grant. I love you but I was too scared to admit it, even to myself."

"And you're not scared anymore?"

"Now that I know just how madly in love with me you are, no way!" it was true what they said about love giving you strength you didn't know you possessed. "Now I can shout it out loud, I love you Grant Lopez!"

His deep laugh sounded loud as it reverberated against my chest, producing a shiver than ran the length of my body. "Say it again." His words were intense behind the command and I knew it mattered to him.

"I love you Grant. I love you and I love Mariana."

"And one day in the future, I'm gonna ask you to move in with us, to make our family official and you'll say?"

"Heck yeah!" I tossed my head back and laughed, loving the way Grant kept a tight, protective grip on me so I was never in danger of falling. "But it should be a ways into the future, don't' you think? Wouldn't want to set a bad example for Mari, would we?"

His lips were on mine in an instant, hot and sweet and deep, he poured everything he was feeling into that kiss. I accepted it all with a shuddery sigh as I clung to his shoulders. "I really do love you, Brenna."

"You already said that."

"I mean it."

"Good, because you're stuck with me."

"Forever?"

"If you can handle forever with me, I'm willing to give you forever, Grant."

"Oh, I can handle it." With a hungry smile, Grant picked me up in his arms and carried me upstairs where he spent most of the night showing me just how eager he was to get started on our very own forever after.

THE END

Check out the other books in this series!
Scan the QR code below for more.

FOREVER CURVES

PREVIEW: HERO IN MY BED

She's beautiful, perfect, and most importantly, she's mine.
She just doesn't know it yet.

I need to stay away from the town's hot golden boy.

He's *waaaay* out my league.

That doesn't mean I can't have my dirty fantasies though, right?

I know I can't have him.

But we're forced to work on the town's charity calendar, and we end up roommates.

Unable to escape each other.

I try to resist him.

To forget the way he makes me feel when I'm pressed against his hard body.

But I'm losing the fight.

And when he kisses me?

I know I'm screwed.

My only solace is that it will only be for a couple of days.
But Preston...
Let's just say he has other plans for me.

CHAPTER 1
NINA

Some people might think working as a bartender in a small-town bar would give me the inside track on all the gossip that could be found in a town the size of Tulip, Texas.

Those people would be wrong, though. As it turns out, booze does not loosen lips nearly as effectively as a stare-down from a blue-haired old lady. That's right — all the gossip was carefully released in a steady trickle by a group of three old women ranging in age from seventy-something to the high end of eighty.

At twenty-five, I didn't qualify for their inner circle, never mind that I was an outsider who'd only been a resident of Tulip for the past seven months. Who knew how long it would take before I became a local, not that I'd planned to stick around that long.

Maybe.

It was late afternoon and the Black Thumb was mostly empty, now that the lunch rush was over. But Janey Matheson, photographer extraordinaire, held court at one of the booths that split the restaurant seating area from the pool tables, dartboards, and foosball tables. And since the daytime waitresses had all left after counting their tips, it was up to me to make sure her crowd received their pitcher of margaritas and round of tequila shots.

"Here we go, ladies," I announced, unloading my tray onto the table.

"Thanks, Nina." Janey flashed a bright smile, her perky ponytail bouncing just from the force of her words. "Hey, would you sign up to be part of a bachelor and bachelorette auction? It's for a good cause."

I frowned back at her cheerful face. As nice as the people in Tulip were, they were also manipulative as hell. One kind word, and you were signed up to judge a meatloaf cooking contest and a senior beauty pageant.

"Hell, no. Guys can be weird and creepy and totally pervy. Best to put the control and the bidding in the hands of women."

She beamed another smile my way, dimples winking from both cheeks, giving her a girl-next-door appeal I was sure the men of Tulip appreciated. "You are a genius, Nina. An absolute genius."

I mean, *I* thought so but, big surprise, so did Janey. "You said bartender wrong," I deadpanned, which for some reason made all the women at the table erupt in laughter. "Besides, I'm more of a look-but-don't-touch kind of girl when it comes to men."

Janey's raven brows rose in surprise. "So, you're... celibate?" She gasped, as though the idea was so far-fetched that she just couldn't believe it.

"Since I moved here, yeah. And I'm fine with that."

Honestly, I was. Sure, men had their purpose, but so far I hadn't found one worth keeping, and until I did, celibacy was fine with me. "Batteries can do wonders for a girl's disposition."

She tapped her chin, her gaze thoughtful. "You do make a valid point, but men are just so big and strong and… delicious." As Janey seemed lost in her own thoughts, I started to wonder if there was anyone in particular who put that wistful look on her face. "Oh. My. God. You really *are* a genius, Nina!"

I let that compliment sink in, because I didn't get them all that often from anyone other than myself. "You're going to sell vibrators, instead of the men of Tulip?"

For the past three months, everyone in town over the age of fifteen had been trying to come up with the perfect fundraiser to repair the town center's statue-fountain-garden structure, which featured the town founder Tulip Worthington.

"No, we're going to do a calendar. A big ol' beefcake calendar, showing off the men of Tulip."

I shrugged. "I'd buy one." As the saying went, they grew 'em big down in Texas and the men here seemed to be especially big, even for Texas.

"Oh, this is good. *So* good," Janey muttered to herself, whipping out a red, white, and blue notebook with a cover that looked like a pair of distressed jeans. After a minute or two of furious writing, she was on her feet and rushing out the door.

I turned to the rest of the women and grinned. "Let me know if you ladies need anything else."

"Salt, please."

"Coming right up." The thing I loved most about Texas was how friendly and open everyone was. Sure, I was still an outsider, but the people here said 'please' and 'thanks' automatically, never making me feel like the service worker I was.

The doors flew open and Janey breezed back in, smacking a couple twenty-dollar bills on the bar with a wide smile. "Sorry, and thanks." Then, she was gone again, leaving the Black Thumb just a little quieter and dimmer than before.

My three occupied tables all had drinks while they waited for their late lunch orders to arrive. I slid behind the bar and busied myself with the boring part of my job – wiping down the counters, restocking empty bottles of booze, and checking the levels on the kegs.

The last task I needed to finish before my shift ended was cutting more garnish for the cocktails the good people of Tulip rarely ordered. But I liked working at the Black Thumb and I liked my boss, Buddy, even if he was a bit crusty and grouchy sometimes. So, I did all the tasks assigned to me without complaining.

Mostly.

"Hey, Nina, isn't your shift over already?" Buddy pushed through the swinging door off the side of the bar, leading with his gut – the result of years of enjoying too many beers and too much barbecue.

Nodding, I glanced at my watch, even though I already knew the time. "Well, my bear of a boss insists I slice these lemons as thinly as possible, so he can save some cash." I winked and Buddy doubled over with laughter, clutching his big belly until he was red in the face.

"A man don't get rich giving away stuff for free."

"Not even a drop of lemon juice?"

"Especially the little things. They want a real slice of lemon, they can order something other than a beer." It was a familiar refrain, Buddy complaining that his customers preferred cheap beer to the pricey beverages he offered. "Anyway, I didn't come out here to discuss my business strategy with you, missy."

I laughed, loving the way Buddy sometimes sounded like a librarian from the fifties. "Okay. Want to tell me why you came out, then?"

A smile that looked suspiciously like trouble crossed his face. "To remind you that you're off this weekend. Heard you got roped into helping with the Tulip's Troops annual camping trip."

Yeah, I had, and roped was exactly the right word to use. It had been a sneak attack from the one and only friend I'd made during my time in town, and somehow, I'd volunteered for the task of spending the weekend with a bunch of little girls.

"I did, and I didn't forget." I had hoped one of the attractive-but-unreliable waitresses Buddy favored would call off, but it appeared luck was not on my side.

"I'm still trying to figure out how you got them to overlook that ring in your nose and the ink on your arm," he said with a shake of his head in the direction of the colorful sleeve of tattoos traveling up my right arm.

It was a mystery to me, too. "I wish they *would* fear me, just enough that I stopped getting roped into these things."

Not that I minded much, but it always seemed to highlight my status as an outsider, as well another thing I didn't have. Family.

Buddy smacked his thigh with a laugh. "No way honey, now that they know what a soft touch you are, you're a goner. Welcome to Tulip, Nina. Now, get on out of here and enjoy the rest of your night. Maybe go out on a date or get laid, as you young people say."

I exaggerated my frown. "Laid? What's that?"

He grinned, shooing me toward the door. "Hush up and wash that apron."

"I'll do it tonight, before my date with Netflix and Reese's Famous BBQ."

"That's the most pathetic thing I've ever heard," Buddy teased. "Just wait until the blue hairs hear you're still single."

Sheriff Henderson was considerately holding the door open for me to exit, so I resisted the urge to flip Buddy the bird as I took off for the night. "Evening, Sheriff."

"Evenin', Miss Nina." He was as polite as he was handsome. And quiet. In fact, he'd be perfect for Janey's calendar.

CHAPTER 2
PRESTON

"Wanna grab a beer tonight?" Nate Callahan asked me as we left the Search & Rescue offices on the top floor of Tulip's Emergency Services building.

"Maybe. I'll let you know, but right now, I'm beat." Search and rescue shifts were similar to fire departments — Nate and I worked three days straight with two days off, which sounded worse than it was since most of the time was spent watching for fire hazards and reposting signs.

"Beat? We had one rescue and it was two experienced hikers. What has you so tired, a woman?" Nate looked over at me and I saw the hope in his eyes quickly turn to disappointment.

"I'm just tired, that's all. We're not as young as we used to be, you know."

Nate laughed. "Speak for yourself, old man. If you change your mind, I'll be at the Black Thumb by nine. And if

I don't see you there, I'll pray that you're wrapped around some fine young thing."

"Bless you," I replied sarcastically and groaned as we stepped outside. My older brother Grant was leaning against my blue Escalade, a vehicle which made me stick out like a sore thumb here in pickup truck country.

"Good luck with that," Nate said, nodding in my brother's direction. "If you do need a drink, or ten, my spare room is yours."

"Thanks, Nate. See you bright and early Saturday morning."

He sighed at the reminder of our early clock-in time, the same way he always did. "Don't remind me!"

My good mood lasted exactly as long as it took me to reach my ride. "I'm too tired for your games today, Grant."

My brother pushed off the front of the car and smoothed the sides of his designer suit, probably chosen by our mother. "Good, because I'm not here for games."

"Yeah? Then why are you here?" I couldn't remember the last time he'd stopped by to see me without an ulterior motive.

"Mom wants to see you for Sunday dinner this week."

There it was. "Then she should call and invite me," I retorted. "Or, I don't know, maybe learn my work schedule."

Which was exactly what I'd been telling our mother since she'd informed me that I was no longer part of the family, after I'd chosen S&R over law school. Not that it mattered — without an apology, I still did exactly what was expected of someone bearing the Worthington name, which meant presenting a united, picture-perfect front in public. But when it came to family get-togethers, I didn't waste my time with my own, opting instead to spend time with my best friend Ry's big group of boisterous relatives.

Grant sighed, like he was the one put out by a visit he'd initiated. "When are you going to let this go? It's getting old."

"If you hate it so much, stop dropping by uninvited." That was the problem with Grant: he thought he was always right. I thought he was just an asshole. "Trust me, these little visits aren't the highlight of my day, either."

"Mom—"

"No. Stop." I put a hand to Grant's chest, so he knew I was serious. "Mom made her decision and she's stuck to it all these years. So have I. If she wants to change things, *Mom* knows what she has to do." I didn't hate my mom, but I didn't like her much either. Even though she was a snob who respected no one's opinion but her own, I'd be willing to try if she offered up a sincere apology. "Now, if that's all you wanted?"

Grant stared at me with blue eyes about two shades lighter than mine, trying to figure me out. It was a waste of time, really, because I was a 'what you see is what you get' kind of guy. "That's all," he said, finally.

"Good. See you around." It was a lie we both told each other, because it wouldn't do for the town's favored sons to be obviously at each other's throats.

The drive home took the same fifteen minutes it always did. There was never any traffic this time of day, and few people lived on the edge of town, if they could help it. But to me, the southern edge of Tulip was perfect, and when Gary Strange had put the lot up for sale a few years back, I'd bought it and built a place overlooking the picturesque lake.

"Home sweet home." Inside the front door, I kicked off my boots and stripped down as I made my way to the bathroom. It was kind of ritualistic for me, taking a hot shower after a long shift to help gauge if I was truly exhausted or just too tired to deal with people. Even after stepping out of the steaming bathroom and changing into something more comfortable than my S&R uniform, I knew I wasn't quite ready to hit the sack, so I grabbed a couple beers and went out to my deck. To relax.

Watching the calm waters of the lake had a soothing effect on me, which I needed after another run-in with Grant the self-appointed peacekeeper of the family. It was a role he'd excelled in, until I'd thrown the proverbial wrench in our family's plan for me to, eventually, become lead counsel for Worthington Enterprises. Since then, things had broken down so much there was no longer any peace to be kept.

But here, at my home, there was always peace. Mostly because I only issued invites to friends. Close friends. My space wasn't open to women or family.

The sound of the phone ringing on the deck next to my beer broke the spell the lake had slowly begun to cast on me, and I reached over to pick it up. "Yeah?"

"Dude, your phone manners would shock an ape."

I couldn't stop the smile that spread across my face at the sound of my best friend's voice. "Ry, if an ape is calling me, he deserves my bad manners — I don't recall giving my number to any apes."

His loud, barking laugh sounded down the line. "I don't know, Pres. Maybe you've got a new type." The thing I loved about Ry was his ever-present optimism. He didn't let anything in life get him down and, without fail, started every damn day with a smile. It was a trait I admired but had no real desire to emulate. "Drinks tonight at the Black Thumb?"

"Isn't tonight Ladies Night?"

"Exactly. The ladies will show up for half-priced drinks and, by the time we get there, they'll be tipsy enough to stop pretending to be good girls."

I snorted. "We grew up with damn near every woman in town, Ry. Who do you have your eye on?"

"No one in particular." The answer came too fast to be true, but I let it slide. "So, tonight? I have news you'll want to hear."

"I'm all ears now, Ry."

"Fine, stay in the house until your cock shrivels up and dies from lack of use. See if I care."

"My cock appreciates your concern, man."

He snorted, and I could picture his smile — part annoyed and part amused. "Only because you're my brother from another mother will I indulge in any sort of gossip with you."

"Understood."

"Word around town is that Sabrina Worthington is engaging in a bit of matchmaking, inviting nearly a dozen women to one of her infamous dinner parties. This Sunday."

I groaned. My mother Sabrina only had two children with James Worthington, my dad: Grant who was dating one of the governor's daughters, and me. Painfully, permanently single me. "That makes sense. Grant was waiting for me when I got off work, issuing an invite on Mom's behalf. I wondered why."

"Well, now we know. Preston will soon be off the market." Ry's voice boomed loudly, a sure sign that he was either alone or in the presence of one of his three sisters, who loved to pretend they had crushes on me.

"Seeing as she hasn't apologized to me, I won't be there on Sunday." And, now that I knew what her motives were, I'd make sure to be busy. "Work."

"I feel your pain, man, I really do. Even if you would be doing me a solid by going to this party and getting some numbers for me. These chicks are rich, right?"

I laughed. Ry talked a big game, but he was the proverbial nice guy. "You can go in my place, since Mom will definitely have a place setting for me." So few people went against her wishes, she'd grown to expect that the whole world would bow down at her bidding.

"I'd rather have you do the heavy lifting."

I wouldn't be doing any lifting. I'd be at work on Sunday until late in the afternoon, and then I would sleep at least ten hours. And there would be no husband-hunters to be seen. "If you don't show up in my place, you'll have to make it happen with Lefty and Righty."

Ry barked out a laugh that was way too loud and way too amused for my liking. "I always find a way. So, am I gonna see you at the Black Thumb tonight?"

I glanced down at the beer in my hand and at the other dripping condensation on the wooden slats next to me before I turned my gaze back to the lake, smiling. "Nah. I'm fine right where I am."

CHAPTER 3
NINA

Early mornings were the worst, even in a beautiful place like Tulip. But I had already agreed to this damn camping trip, which, for some reason, had to take place at the absolute ass crack of dawn. Why did I do this to myself? I knew the answer — Buddy had said it a few days ago. I was a softy. Despite my best efforts, with my badass 'don't fuck with me' persona, the ink and the piercings, I was a big ol' softy.

That, and the fact that these people were genuinely nice. Annoyingly nice, even, which made it hard to be a bitch to anyone and even harder to say no. Which is exactly how I found myself walking up First Street, Tulip's answer to Main Street, before the sun even rose.

But I wasn't prepared for a weekend filled with seven- to nine-year-old girls. Or a weekend spent in the woods. Serial killers and other crazies didn't avoid places because they were part of the National Parks System.

Walking along First Street, right down the middle of the

road, I took in the quiet beauty of the town. Brick sidewalks gave Tulip's downtown a welcoming, cozy feel, which was enhanced by colorful awnings announcing the quirky names of locally-owned businesses. There was the diner, Big Mama's Place, where you could get the best scrambled eggs on the planet. Next door was the Bloomin' Tulip Bookstore, which had been around since well before e-books were a thing, and its bright rainbow awning often gave people the wrong impression. Tulip boasted two small women's boutiques, side by side, just before you got to Bo's General Store, where you could find everything from farming equipment to blue jeans, gas grills to Brie.

It was truly a picture-perfect small town, with trimmed trees along the streets adorned with twinkle lights that flickered on as the sun's light grew dim and oversized flowerpots beside the entrances to each business. And, of course, the statue of Tulip Worthington, though it hadn't fared well during the tornado that blew through town at the start of spring.

Tulip had been a pioneer in her own right, running away from home at the age of sixteen to avoid marrying a man twice her age she didn't love. She'd thought of heading west, as many people had done at the time, but had stopped to regroup in this part of Texas and never left, after falling in love with a local farmer and helping him turn a little flower operation into what was now a multi-million dollar corporation. At least, that was the story I'd been told.

Over and over again.

Ad nauseum.

But Tulip was looking a little worse for wear — the

statue, as well as the fountain and garden surrounding it, was in desperate need of a makeover.

Soon, ol' girl. Soon.

As I approached the meet-up spot just beyond Tulip's statue, I ducked into Bo's for a very large cup of coffee.

"Mornin' Nina!" Bo waved, her thick brown hair falling silkily around her shoulders. Her blue eyes were sparkling too brightly for this time of the morning.

"Hey Bo, how's it going?"

"Not too bad. Not yet, anyway. Coffee? I just got in this new hazelnut stuff that people seem to love." She chuckled to herself as she reached for a cup and the pot of coffee behind her. "Cass refuses to get the flavored stuff, so I figured this wasn't cutting in on her business."

"Any business that can't handle a little competition is a business that will soon fail." I'd heard that enough from different employers over the years to know it was true. "And make that coffee as big as you've got. Please."

With a soft, feminine laugh, Bo set out a large disposable cup and began to pour. "Ready for your weekend in the woods?"

"You heard about that too, huh? Well, I'm not ready, not even a little bit. What if I lose a kid or something?"

"There will be other mothers with you, plus the Tulip Troop Leader. You'll be fine."

I had my doubts, but I kept them to myself and busied myself grabbing a few snack items that would make the perfect bribes for good behavior this weekend. "I guess we'll find out soon enough."

After I paid for my loot, I hurried back outside before someone thought the new chick had flaked on her responsibilities. I wasn't the first person to arrive, but thankfully, I also wasn't the last.

A few moms huddled together over coffee while their girls chatted excitedly near the bright blue school bus rented to take us to our camping spot, or close to it. I didn't know any of the women well enough to offer anything more than a wave and a nod in greeting, so I started loading my gear.

"Hey Nina, glad you could make it."

I smiled as I backed out of the seat I'd chosen all the way in the back of the bus, turning in the direction of my friend Max's voice. "I'm here," I confirmed, "and I'm prepared for just about anything."

Maxine Nash had been the first person to befriend me on my second day in Tulip. With curly red hair, big green eyes, and enough curves to make Sofia Vergara jealous, Max was a vibrant single mother who cooked the best food I'd ever had the fortune of tasting. "You'll be fine. The girls love you and they listen to you, which puts my mind at ease."

As the official leader of the Tulip Buds, the name assigned to the youngest group of Tulip's Troops, the safety of everyone involved in this trip fell on Max's shoulders — which is how I got roped into this in the first place.

While I had my doubts about the girls, with plenty of other moms around I figured I was the designated fun grownup. By the time the bus was loaded with gear and the girls, though, tension started to creep in.

As we left the town of Tulip behind and the girls were on their thirtieth bottle of perfume on the wall, I was dancing on the edges of a full-blown panic attack. It was a special kind of torture, one that ended only when the bus came to a stop in one of the parking lots outside the seemingly endless national park.

"Thank god," I whispered to Max, who shook her head with a soft chuckle.

"That wasn't too painful, right?"

Easy for her to say, since she was used to the chaos of having kids around. Between her adorable daughter and her friends, the stress of being a caterer and business owner, Max thrived on challenge. I, on the other hand, had been alone for most of my life — this kind of activity was new to me.

After my father died, my mom spent less and less time at home, until finally, she just stopped coming home altogether. My Uncle Rudy stepped in and raised me from the time I was seven until he died after I turned twelve.

I spent the next three years bouncing from foster home to foster home, dealing with money grubbers, perverts, abusers, and the occasional genuine people before I called it quits. Unwilling to continue being tangled up in the system, I stayed under the radar for a few years, got my GED, and left St. Louis behind for good. So yeah, my life was mostly quiet, and this was… not.

"Not if you gave birth to one of the little tone-deaf divas, I suppose."

"What about me, Nina?" Max's seven-year-old daughter looked up at me with big brown eyes, her lopsided red ponytail swinging behind her. "Am I tone deaf, too?"

Callie was quite possibly the cutest little girl in town, with that generous sprinkling of freckles dusted across her nose and cheeks. "I heard one voice that sounded pretty damn good." She gasped at my language, and I shrugged as I crouched down to bring my face level with hers. "I thought it was me, at first, but then I remembered I can't sing, so it must've been you."

"Really?" The awe in her voice gripped my heart and I smiled.

"Yep. I'm sorry to have to tell you that you have terrible taste in music though, squirt."

She laughed. "Hey, I'm a kid. You can't say that!"

"I just did. Now, grab your gear so we can get this show on the road."

Not that Callie or any of the other buds offered much help when it came to putting up tents or setting up camp, but they were the troops and we had to let them earn their badges.

Or try, anyway.

I'd only been at this camping thing for about six hours, but other than a headache, things were going well. Two girls were on time-out in their tents for mocking Bailey, a quiet seven-year-old with white-blond hair who had just moved to town.

Was it wrong to call nine-year-old girls, bitches? Probably, so I kept the thought to myself.

The kids sat around the fire in groups of two or three, chatting with more animation than any human needed. Max and Callie were huddled together, watching another girl working on getting a smaller fire going. Bailey sat on the other side of the big fire, all alone, so I figured I'd better set a good example by trying to include her. "Hey kid, what are you doing here all by yourself?"

She shrugged, barely looking up as I took a seat on the log beside her. "Just watchin'."

"I know what you mean."

"You do?" She looked over at me cautiously.

I nodded. "Of course, I do. I moved here recently too, and it's hard to find out where you belong in a place where the people have known each other since the day they were born."

"I'm not good at making friends," Bailey confessed.

"Me, either. Max was the first person to befriend me." She'd accosted me in the grocery store, looking for someone to act as a guinea pig for her new recipes. From then on, she hadn't let me get away with *not* being part of the community.

"Callie, too," Bailey said sadly. She was a shy girl who probably relied on having friendly, outgoing friends more than she should. "I like your tattoos."

"Thanks, you're one of the few people around here who does." Everyone stared. Half of them probably thought I was some disgraced biker chick, but they were far too polite to say it out loud. "What badges do you plan to earn this weekend, Bailey?"

She shrugged. "I already know how to start a fire, so I guess first aid, environmental stewardship, and nature identification?"

"You guess?"

"Yeah. I'm good at following directions, but some of them need you to have a buddy and I don't have one. Callie and Toni are already buddies."

Well, shit. How did parents walk around all the time with their hearts bleeding and breaking for their kids? "Then I guess we'll be buddies, and that's good news for you — I don't need any badges. You can teach me all this stuff and probably get yourself some kind of teacher badge."

Bailey giggled, but her face still looked serious. "Thank you."

"Anytime, kid. Now, let's get over there before all the marshmallows are gone." I stood and held out my hand, waiting patiently because I knew exactly what it meant to be a stubborn little kid. Plus, I was pretty confident I could out stubborn her any day of the week. "Well?"

"Fine." Sighing, she took my hand and let me tug her to the other side of the campfire where she grabbed two sticks, marshmallows, and s'mores ingredients.

Then, she retired back to the other side of the fire. I grinned. Bailey was my kind of kid.

CHAPTER 4
PRESTON

Days off were precious to me, because of how the NPS configured schedules. Working three days on with two days off meant I had to get everything — including cleaning, shopping, running errands, and even doctor's appointments — done in those two days. There was no relaxing on my days off until all the busy work was out of the way.

Today was a rare full day of no work — I'd gotten everything done yesterday, which meant the entire day was mine. I didn't plan to do a damn thing, other than watch TV and maybe finish building the bookshelf I'd started months ago.

Even *that* was a big fat maybe.

But the sound of the doorbell over the hard rock music blaring from my stereo put a major kink in my plans. Resisting the temptation to pretend I didn't hear it, I pulled the door open to see Ry standing on the front porch. "What are you doing here?"

"Good to see you too, butthead." He punched my

shoulder and walked right inside, like it was his house instead of mine — something we'd been doing since we were boys. "I figured you were over here wallowing, and I thought you might want some company."

"Not really." I grinned at Ry as he surveyed the room. "But, since you brought beer, you can stay."

"Gee, thanks." His sardonic tone pulled a smile from me and he glanced around the living room at the empty pizza box and beer bottles that littered the coffee table. "Look at this dump. Your anal retentiveness must be on the fritz," he teased, pounding on my back like it was an old school TV.

"Stop that." I smacked his hand away and he laughed, following me to the kitchen. "I wasn't in a cleaning mood this weekend, sue me."

"It's not like you can't afford a cleaning lady."

"You know why I don't." My trust fund had been released when I turned twenty-five and, since it had been put in place by my grandfather, mom couldn't use it to punish me or manipulate me to get her way.

"I *know*, but I still don't understand." Ry shook his head, but dropped the subject. "Maybe you could get me a cleaning lady, then? My birthday is coming up."

"In, like, six months," I shot back and made my way to the kitchen.

"Still coming up," he explained with a shrug and shoved the six pack in the fridge, pulling out two already cold beers and handing one to me. "You really aren't going to your mom's dinner party this weekend?"

Everyone in Tulip knew about Sabrina Worthington's infamous dinner parties and thought it was a privilege to get an invite. Me excluded.

"If Mom can so easily dismiss me from the family for my choices, she can be a damned adult and apologize if she wants our relationship to change. Until that happens, I'll only show up to public events."

"You think the town doesn't notice?"

I was sure they did; the main currency in Tulip was gossip. "You think I care?" It had hurt at first, admittedly, that one little difference of opinion had pretty much cost me my family, but as time wore on, the pain had turned to anger and frustration to the point that it had stopped mattering to me. "Besides, I'm happy where I am."

"Are you?"

"Hell, yes. All those charity functions where more money goes to putting on the event than to the actual charity, the gorgeous empty shells of women groomed to become trophy wives, the constant talk of business, vacations, and material bullshit — no, thank you."

"Let's go back to these gorgeous empty shells for a moment."

We both laughed at that, having experienced our fair share of girls "slumming it" with men they'd never consider husband material: an EMT and a search and rescue worker.

"Did you finally strike out with little miss mysterious?" Ry's mystery crush had him all tied up, but he still wouldn't say anything about her. Trying to guess her identity had become my favorite pastime.

"Nah, she's going out of town this weekend. Soon though, I'll ask her."

"You've been saying that for months." Ry glared at me and I chuckled, nodding toward the back deck. "Come on, those steaks aren't gonna cook themselves."

Ry pushed past me to the spice rack his baby sister had given me as a housewarming gift. "Thank goodness for Shelby or we'd be eating plain beef." He pulled out a few small glass bottles and sprinkled various seasonings on both sides of the meat before pushing it aside. "I know you have fries in the freezer; pop'em into the oven."

I knew the drill. This was our routine whenever we hung out: steak and fries, with beer on my deck. "Happy, chef?"

"Ecstatic. So, tell me how the Worthington clan is handling the fact that the whole town wants to help repair Tulip's Tribute?"

"No clue. Contrary to what my mother thinks, the entire world doesn't revolve around what she wants. Besides, the town council took it out of her hands," I told him with a smile. "Probably because she thinks throwing money at every problem puts her in charge of it all."

"Including your love life."

"Especially that," I groaned. Just thinking about her interference pissed me off. "This dinner party will be the perfect time for her to learn another valuable lesson — if I do choose to settle down, it will be with a woman *I* choose for reasons *I* deem important."

Besides, how Mom thought she could get one of her society girls to marry a man who wore a uniform to work and climbed rough terrain for a living was beyond me.

"You know she thinks you'll give in at the last minute? She said as much to the Potluck Patrol." That was the name we'd given to the trio of town gossips who were the first to show up on your doorstep to welcome you, console you, or celebrate your achievements with various potluck offerings.

"I can't worry about what my mom thinks or I'll actually lose my mind."

"Well, how about a different mom?" Ry offered. "Mine's having a barbecue next weekend and she's demanding your famous sweet potato salad, along with your presence."

I had to smile as my head nodded automatically. Betty Kemp was the mother I always wanted. At five-foot-nothing and weighing a buck oh five, she was bossier than any CEO or drill sergeant. "I'll be there."

"Maybe I ought to have Ma share her secrets with Sabrina."

"Do it and I'll put super glue in your shampoo."

Ry frowned and raked a hand through his thick brown wavy hair — his pride and joy. "You fight dirty."

"Don't you forget it," I confirmed, aiming the tongs his way.

"Like I could," he said, raising a dramatic hand to his side. "I still have the scars to prove it."

"First of all, we were twelve. And you lost your balance."

His lips twitched; he knew it was true. "That's revisionist history and you know it. You totally pushed me."

"I tried to save your dumb ass!" I'd nearly fallen from that same tree in my effort to keep Ry from dropping about twenty feet to his death. Luckily, he'd only ended up with a badly broken arm. "And, if I recall, that cast got you a date with Mary Sue Markham."

Ry smiled broadly, his gaze wistful. "Yeah, that was a damn good three weeks. One more and I'd have gotten some boob action."

I pulled open the doors that led to *my* pride and joy — the teak deck I'd spent a full month building, sanding, and staining. "If you want, I can break your arm again and you can get another three weeks with Mary Sue. I hear she's between husbands right now."

Ry shuddered as he pulled open the lid of the grill and started it up. "No thanks. She's way too fertile, and I can't see myself with Mary Sue in sickness and in health and all that crap."

"And the ladies say romance is dead," I teased. He flipped me off and grabbed the steaks, tossing them on the hot grill. "Can't imagine why they're not flocking to you."

"Yeah? You're rich, buddy, and they're not flocking to you, either."

"Thank goodness for that." The last thing I needed was a repeat of college and the subsequent year of law school, with eager coeds looking to land a rich husband. It was exhausting, fending them off and trying to figure out if a girl was into me for me or just for the money I would inherit a few years after graduation. "When I'm ready, I'll find a girl."

Ry smirked, closing the lid on the grill as he popped open his beer and took a long slug. "Or maybe, she'll find you."

"In this town full of women I've known since birth? Unlikely."

"Famous last words, my friend. Famous last words."

Nina & Preston's story continues...
Scan the QR code below for more.

PREVIEW: HERO IN MY BED

ALSO BY PIPER SULLIVAN

Small Town Lovers

Midlife Baby: Morgot & Grady

Midlife Fake Out: Bella & Derek

Midlife Love Affair: Lacy & Levi

Midlife Valentine: Valona & Trey

Midlife Do Over: Pippa & Ryan

Healing Love

Dueling Drs, Book 6: Zola & Drew

Rockstar Baby Daddy, Book 5: Susie & Gavin

Unfriending the Dr, Book 4: Persy & Ryan

Kissing the Dr, Book 3: Megan & Casey

Loving the Nurse, Book 2: Gus & Antonio

Falling for the Dr, Book 1: Teddy & Cal

Curvy Girl Dating Agency

Forever Curves, Book 8: Brenna & Grant

Small Town Curves, Book 7: Shannon & Miles

Curvy Valentine Match, Book 6: Mara & Xander

Misbehaving Curves, Book 5: Joss & Ben

Curves for the Single Dad, Book 4: Tara & Chris

His Curvy Best Friend, Book 3: Sophie & Stone

Curvy Girl's Secret, Book 2: Olive & Liam

His Curvy Enemy, Book 1: Eva & Oliver

Small Town Protectors (Tulip Series)

That Hot Night, Book 12: Janey & Rafe

To Catch A Player, Book 11: Reece & Jackson

Cold Hearted Love, Book 10: Ginger & Tyson

Hero Boss, Book 9: Stevie & Scott

Dr's Orders, Book 8: Maxine & Derek

Mastering Her Curves, Book 7: Mikki & Nate

Kissing My Best Friend, Book 6: Bo & Jase

Undesired, Book 5: Hope & Will

Wanting Ms Wrong, Book 4: Audrey & Walker

Loving My Enemy, Book 3: Elka & Antonio

Bad Boy Benefits, Book 2: Penny & Ry

Hero In My Bed, Book 1: Nina & Preston

Accidental Hookups

Accidentally Hitched, Book 1: Viviana & Nash

Accidentally Wed, Book 2: Maddie & Zeke

Accidentally Bound, Book 3: Trish & Mason

Accidentally Wifed, Book 4: Magenta & Davis

Boardroom Games

His Takeover: An Enemies to Lovers Romance (Boardroom Games Book 1)

Sinful Takeover: An Enemies to Lovers Romance (Boardroom Games Book 2)

Naughty Takeover: An Enemies to Lovers Romance (Boardroom Games 3)

Boxsets & Collections

Small Town Misters: A Small Town Protectors Boxset

Misters of Pleasure: A Small Town Protectors Boxset

Misters of Love: A Small Town Romance Boxset

Misters of Passion: A Small Town Romance Boxset

Kiss Me, Love Me: An Alpha Male Romance Boxset

Accidentally On Purpose: A Marriage Mistake Boxset

Daddies & Nannies: A Contemporary Romance Boxset

Cowboys & Bosses: A Contemporary Romance Boxset

About the Author

Piper Sullivan is an old school romantic who enjoys reading romantic stories as much as she enjoys writing them.

She spends her time day-dreaming of dashing heroes and the feisty women they love.

Visit Piper's website www.pipersullivan.com

Join Piper's Newsletter for quirky commentary, new romance releases, freebies and contests.

Check her out on BookBub

Stalk her on Facebook

www.ingramcontent.com/pod-product-compliance
Ingram Content Group UK Ltd.
Pitfield, Milton Keynes, MK11 3LW, UK
UKHW040904090226
10577UKWH00017B/224